### *"Can you answer one question?"*

Devan froze. It had been six years since she'd felt such a mix of emotions, and she was terrified of what he would ask next. Once, she'd made herself his for the taking. She'd risked everything to hear him speak to her and her alone…touch her as she'd never been touched…encourage her to be free, to be truly herself.

But just as he'd changed, she had, too.

She turned back to him. "What?"

"Did you know me? I mean really? Were we… friends?"

Friends? For a night, he'd been everything she could dream of wanting or needing….

# WHAT SHOULD HAVE BEEN

## *HELEN R. MYERS*

*Silhouette*

## SPECIAL EDITION®

Published by Silhouette Books

America's Publisher of Contemporary Romance

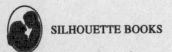

SILHOUETTE BOOKS

ISBN 0-373-24758-3

WHAT SHOULD HAVE BEEN

Visit Silhouette Books at www.eHarlequin.com

Printed in U.S.A.

## Books by Helen R. Myers

**Silhouette Special Edition**

*After That Night...* #1066
*Beloved Mercenary* #1162
*What Should Have Been* #1758

**Silhouette Romance**

*Donovan's Mermaid* #557
*Someone To Watch Over Me* #643
*Confidentially Yours* #677
*Invitation to a Wedding* #737
*A Fine Arrangement* #776
*Through My Eyes* #814
*Three Little Chaperones* #861
*Forbidden Passion* #908
*A Father's Promise* #1002
*To Wed at Christmas* #1049
*The Merry Matchmaker* #1121
*\*Baby in a Basket* #1169

*\*Daddy Knows Last*

**Silhouette Books**

*Silhouette Shadows Collection* 1992
"Seawitch"

**Montanta Mavericks**
*The Law Is No Lady* #8

**Silhouette Desire**

*Partners for Life* #370
*Smooth Operator* #454
*That Fontaine Woman!* #471
*The Pirate O'Keefe* #506
*Kiss Me Kate* #570
*After You* #599
*When Gabriel Called* #650
*Navarrone* #738
*Jake* #797
*Once Upon a Full Moon* #857
*The Rebel and the Hero* #941
*Just a Memory Away* #990
*The Officer and the
   Renegade* #1102

**Silhouette Shadows**

*Night Mist* #6
*Whispers in the Woods* #23
*Watching for Willa* #49

**MIRA Books**

*Come Sundown*
*More Than You Know*
*Lost*
*Final Stand*
*No Sanctuary*
*While Others Sleep*

## HELEN R. MYERS

a collector of two- and four-legged strays, lives deep in the Piney Woods of East Texas. She cites cello music and bonsai gardening as favorite relaxation pastimes, and still edits in her sleep—an accident learned while writing her first book. The bestselling author of diverse themes and focus, she is a three-time RITA® Award nominee, winning for *Navarrone* in 1993.

To my dear friend
Darese Cotton

This one's for you because you asked most and loudest

# Chapter One

*"Mommy!"*

Blakeley's cry had Devan dropping the hot pan of garlic bread onto the kitchen counter. Ripping off her new sunflower pot-holder mittens, she threw them after it, sending one skittering off the edge of the granite top, but she let it go. All she cared about was the panic in her child's voice.

By the time she yanked open the back door, Blakeley was scrambling across the stone patio. At the same time she flung herself into Devan's arms, the little girl also locked all four limbs around her and clutched handfuls of her glittery autumn-motif sweatshirt.

"Sweetie, what on earth…? What's wrong?"

"There's a man out there! A stranger in *my* park!"

For once Devan didn't correct or reprove her four-year-old daughter for her habit of calling everything she had a personal attachment to as "mine." Instead she lifted her gaze to confirm that the back gate on the chain-link fence was open. That was enough to send her imagination into overdrive. She'd warned Blakeley repeatedly never to open the gate on her own, let alone venture beyond it without her—especially into Mount Vance, Texas's woodsy Regan Park. The headstrong minx had inherited too many of her genes, all the wrong ones!

"Are you all right?" she demanded, hugging the child closer until she could feel her small heart through her light red jacket. She inhaled that unforgettable but fading baby scent to help calm her own pounding heart. "Did he touch you? Try to hurt you?"

"No." Blakeley's voice wobbled with emotion. "Because I ran. He scared me, Mommy. He just stood on the other side of the creek and stared."

She'd gotten as far as the creek? Devan couldn't believe she had let her out of her sight for that long without glancing outside. Her impulse was to dial 911, but she reminded herself that in the meantime, the creep could be getting away. She needed to find him, to see if she could identify him. The police would need an accurate description.

Just then the front door opened and her mother-in-law Connie poked her head inside. Devan had left the door unlocked expecting her at any minute to pick up a box of outgrown children's clothing for a church fund-raiser this weekend.

Setting down Blakeley, Devan grabbed her jacket from the hanger behind the back door and called, "Connie, lock the door and call 911! Blakeley, tell Nana what you told me. Lock this door, too."

"Where are you going?" Blakeley cried, her blue eyes huge.

"I promise I'll be right back, sweetie. Now do as I say."

Planting a kiss on top of Blakeley's blond head, Devan grabbed Jay's old baseball bat, which she always took on walks in the park against the threat of some stray, sick dog attacking them. Then she rushed from the house, ignoring Connie's protest and her daughter's whimpering; she ran across the yard, and alley, and entered the woods marking the east boundary of their neighborhood.

Regan Park framed Regan Creek, land donated by one of the most powerful families in the northeast Texas county. Barely an acre wide and eighteen long, parts of the outer perimeter were deceptively brushy, but the bike trails were well tended, as were the picnic areas. Often used by joggers and weekend cyclists, at odd hours it had been known to be the rendezvous site of occasional drug deals.

*I should have put a lock on the gate.*

*I didn't even ask her what the guy looked like.*

As she berated herself, Devan charged through the thicket of holly and prickly vines, then between stately pines and bushy cedar. She willed the creep who'd scared her baby to still be out there. She could and *would* stop him—at least long enough to make sure the police were given an excellent description, and to give the man an earful. That scumbag would know what awaited him if he messed with any youngster in Mount Vance.

After another few yards she crossed the bike and jogging trail, but when she came in view of the creek, she stumbled to a halt. At first she thought the heavy shade cast by a sinking October sun was playing tricks on her. But no, that was a man standing monument-still on the opposite bank just as Blakeley described. More unnerving was who he reminded her of; there was something so familiar about him. With every shallow breath, her impulse to charge and swing receded like the most fleeting dream and left her feeling…what?

"Mead." She'd seen the article in the *Mount Vance Report,* had heard the gossip flooding town like white-water bursting from a broken dam. Most she'd managed to ignore in her struggle to repress the fear that her past could finally have caught up with her. However, there was no hiding from the reality that stood in front of her.

She shifted so what sunlight trickled in through the trees worked to her benefit and drew a steadying breath. She remembered those compelling eyes—dark as the promise of Poe's raven whispering, "Nevermore." Gone was the near-black mane of windswept hair of his youth, though she'd seen it almost this short on his last visit home. The bristles now appeared to be seasoned with a hint of gray, as was his beard. He had been home for more than two weeks, but he looked as though he was still existing on a diet of air and willpower, the latter no doubt force-fed him by his mother. Devan estimated him to be at least twenty pounds lighter than was normal for his strong-boned, six-foot-plus frame. The blue bandana not quite hiding the scar at his right temple suggested one of the reasons why.

Her next step forward was involuntary. "Mead…do you hear me?"

Hunkering deeper into the upturned collar of his denim jacket, he stared into the glistening water as though willing himself to merge with the few inches of cold liquid. But her question finally had him raising his eyes in slow motion.

As their gazes met, she almost believed she saw a slight flicker of something like a dawning, only to wait with a mixture of disappointment and relief when he failed to respond. "So it's true…you don't recognize any of us," she finally said.

He made no reply.

She'd known when he left town six years ago that his first destination would be somewhere dangerous...and the next, and the next. Some sixteen months ago, his luck, and that of his crack commando team had finally run out. On a mission to the Middle East that had made national headlines despite the government's attempts to keep information classified, something went catastrophically wrong, and everyone save Mead had been killed. After that, she'd shut her ears and mind to any more information, and thereafter tried not to think about the Mead Regan who was undergoing operation after operation, was no longer himself, and was reportedly lingering somewhere between "strange" and "scary." Small wonder that Blakeley had been spooked, she thought, sighing inwardly.

"It's...it's good to see you on your feet," she finally added. That was all she could get past the lump in her throat.

"Do I know you?" he said at last.

Like it or not, that stung. She remembered him as a kidder, the guy with the slow, wicked smile and a "come hither" invitation in his eyes, characteristics she'd insisted for years annoyed her...until, eventually, she had been drawn in like so many before her. This Mead's countenance was as gray as the stone it appeared to be chiseled from, his deep-set eyes lacking any visible sign of interest in life let alone curiosity about her. Devan decided it would have been easier to deal with news of his death than this. What hell had he seen? What agony had he suffered to come back this far?

*You do not need to go there.*

"Ah...not really. Sorry to intrude," she replied, taking a step backward. It was definitely time to go. Connie was waiting and Blakeley needed reassuring, she reminded herself as she pivoted to return home.

She barely registered the meaning of water splashing before strong fingers closed around her upper arm. Devan had neither time to protest nor to catch the bat slipping from her damp grasp; she was spun around and had to plant her hands flat against his chest not to fall into him.

"No!" Her cry was torn from some sleeping place inside her and sounded foreign to her ears; she couldn't blame Mead for frowning at her.

"Who are you?"

"Devan. Devan Anderson." Then she grimaced and amended, "You knew me as Devan Shaw." She could tell he was trying to make some association and failing. Under her hands, she felt his heart beating as powerfully and rapidly as hers, and sweat began to stain his headband.

"Are you a reporter?"

Of course that would be what was bothering him most. It made sense that he would naturally shun prying eyes and probing questions. His politically savvy, reputation-conscious mother Pamela would have encouraged that caution, warned him to shun the media first and foremost if she wasn't available to monitor each utterance. Devan didn't want to think about what she would have to say if she heard about this.

"No, I co-own Dreamscapes. It's a florist-nursery-landscape business in town."

"I—I don't..."

His gaze shifted away as though she'd asked him a question about quantum physics. Dear heaven, she hated witnessing this and had to fight a strange pressure in her chest, making it even harder to breathe. "It's all right, Mead. It didn't exist when you left." And she had been only weeks away from changing her name, but that could remain fried with the rest of his memory. Removing her hands and easing from his hold, she strove to get their focus back to priorities. "Mead...you just terrified my daughter."

He glanced back toward the creek as though rousing from a nap. "There was a child...she left."

"No kidding. She ran home scared to death by some guy skulking around. Was that you?"

Slowly he touched his forehead near the angry red scar. "I was walking. I needed air."

Devan refused to let memories or sympathy come before her concern for her precious girl. "Well, could you please walk in your yard until you're more...more yourself?"

"There are walls."

True again, with electronically operated iron gates at the end of the driveway. His mother had long been a person to separate herself from the rest of the world, unless it suited her. Some called her Mount Vance's Liz Taylor. For a man who always enjoyed the outdoors every bit as much as Devan did, that kind of restriction had to be suffocating, and it momentarily eased some of her maternal fury. "You still have to go home," she told him. "Your mother's going to initiate a county-wide search for you if she hasn't already."

Once again she began to leave, retrieved the bat and started worrying about explaining this to the police—not to mention Connie.

"Can you answer one question?"

She froze. It had been six years since she'd felt such a mix of emotions and she was terrified what he would ask next. Once, she'd made herself his for the taking. Frustrated, hurt, infatuated, she'd risked everything to hear him speak to her and her alone...touch her as she'd never been touched...encourage her to be free, to be truly herself.

But just as he'd changed, she had, too.

With no small reluctance, Devan half turned back to him. This time his eyes looked clearer, even curious. "What?"

"Did you know me? I mean, really? Were we...friends?"

His hesitation was as sad as the question was bittersweet. Friends? For a night, he'd been everything she could dream of wanting or needing. By dawn he'd raced away to adventure, violence and catastrophe, leaving her with a scrawled four-word message. *Take care of yourself.*

She didn't want to remember. She was a widow with a small child. Mead had been a mistake, a wild indulgence of her youth. "We didn't have time," she replied, shrugging.

"Why?"

This was getting more difficult by the minute. "Pick a reason. There are several that would do."

"I don't understand."

"I was never in your league." To her dismay that earned her another one of those vacant looks. She pointed to herself with her thumb, "Devan Shaw, small-town girl." Then she pointed to him. "Mead Alcott Regan II." When he failed to indicate he understood the nuances of social status, she drawled, "Your mother will be happy to explain it to you."

Promising herself that this time when she walked away, she would keep going, Devan almost slammed into a police officer.

"Are you all right, ma'am?"

The freckled, flustered young cop was as breathless as she'd been from running. Devan had seen him before in his patrol car but couldn't remember if his name was Billy or Bobby something. The town was growing and the police force with it. He had to be three to five years younger than her thirty.

"I'm fine, Officer—" she glanced at his nameplate "—Denny. Sorry for the false alarm."

"The lady back at your house, Mrs. Anderson, said your little girl escaped an attempted kidnapping?"

Devan's heart plummeted and quickly worked to keep this from mushrooming. "My mother-in-law, Blakeley's grandmother. It's all a misunderstanding, as you can see. This is Mead Regan." She gestured behind her. "Son of Mrs. Pamela Regan."

As expected, the name had considerable effect on the newcomer. The red-faced officer glanced beyond her. "Uh—sir? You okay?"

"Yeah," Mead replied.

When he offered nothing else, Office Denny shifted his attention back to her. "So what happened?"

"My daughter disobeyed me by leaving the yard while I was preparing dinner, and I panicked."

Officer Denny studied her for a long moment. "That's it?"

"Yes."

"You're sure?"

"I'm certain."

Denny refocused on Mead. "Why are you here?"

"I was walking."

"Maybe you should go home, sir." The cop glanced down at Mead's wet shoes and jeans. "Do you need me to call for someone to help—uh, escort you?"

Devan winced and wrapped her arms around her waist. At another time, Mead would have turned the guy into a stuttering fool with a mere look…or sent him off laughing, depending what mood he was in. Now all she heard behind her was the sound of footsteps, splashing water and more footsteps. It was all she could do not to go after him and apologize for her part in causing him this humiliation.

"Mrs. Anderson?"

Accepting she had to play out what she'd started, Devan

nodded and led the way back to her house. To her chagrin, at the alley, Officer Denny bent to pick up the Barbie doll Blakeley had dropped. Devan accepted it with shaking hands; she hadn't seen it when charging into the woods. It was the one Blakeley had received for Christmas.

Clearing her throat, she asked, "What happens now? You won't press charges, will you?"

"It's not up to me, but as you said, it was a misunderstanding."

"Your report, though…these things get out onto the radio and into the newspaper." As she regained her composure, she was thinking of the repercussions that could occur from this—for him as well as her.

"Nothing happened to where names need be used, ma'am."

Devan could see he was thinking, too, concerned about Pamela Regan's attorney breathing down the neck of the department for declaring her military hero son a public nuisance.

"Thank you for your timely response and sensitivity, Officer."

"You take care, ma'am. Keep your little girl in sight."

Devan all but gritted her teeth. "I will."

Officer Denny motioned to another cop in the kitchen doorway. Belatedly, Devan recognized petite Sarah White with her spontaneous smile. Sarah's reputation with kids prompted her to wave, albeit wearily. As the two cops left, Blakeley came running and Devan scooped up the only child she expected to ever have to hug her close.

"I'm sorry, Mommy. "

"I know. It's over."

"The man *was* scary."

It was hard not to defend him. "He's been sick, sweetheart."

"Like flu sick or worst?"

"Worse. And I can't answer that question because Mommy isn't a doctor. In any case, you're the one who needs to do some explaining, young lady. What were you doing going out of the yard without telling me?"

"I heard a kitty."

This wasn't a reassuring answer whether it was the truth or not. "Blakeley, you're allergic to cats. If anything, you should run in the opposite direction of a mewing kitten."

"But she was an orphan and in trouble."

Although "orphan" was a new word in her daughter's vocabulary, and "trouble" sounded adorable as "twubble," Devan studied her for a third reason, wondering if Blakeley had inherited another undesirable gene of hers. The one that could shift one's fantasy world and imagination into over-drive, and fabricate stories way too well? Terrific if you were a writer. Potentially problematic when you were trying to teach your preschooler to always tell you the truth.

"We are going to talk. In the meantime, you don't do anything like this again, understood?"

Blakeley hugged her tighter and added a kiss on her cheek. "I love you."

Devan's heart swelled. "I love you, too, but you're still going to bed tonight without TV."

The child dropped her head limply onto her shoulder. "I figgered as much."

Pressing her lips together so as not to smile, Devan replied, "Can you *figger* it's past time to wash up? Dinner will be ready in a minute…what hasn't turned into bedrock."

"What's bedrock?"

Setting her on her feet, Devan pointed her toward the house. "Get going before I haul you into court and change your name to Jabberwocky."

Giggling, Blakeley ran inside and straight to the bathroom.

Devan followed, shutting and locking the back door, preparing herself for Connie. She adored her late husband's mother and was glad she'd arrived in the nick of time to help, but Mead Regan was the last person she wanted to discuss with her.

"What happened?" the youthful-looking, sixty-two-year-old asked.

With her short frosted hair and hopeful gray eyes, she still turned heads whether cheering for Blakeley at her gymnastics class or mowing the lawn in her size four Capri pants. Devan had been blessed to call her "friend" as well as mom-in-law; however, there was no way *this* friend could ever understand her connection to Mead.

"Nothing," she replied, slipping off her jacket. "An embarrassing misunderstanding, that's all." Her gaze fell on the loaf pan that Connie had placed on a cooling rack. "Thanks for your timing—and your help."

"Don't mention it, dear. I'm glad I was on schedule. But do you mean you didn't see anyone out there?"

"Blakeley ran into Mead Regan," Devan admitted reluctantly. That much would get around town fast enough; to keep it from her would only make her wonder.

"*He* tried to get her?"

Devan quickly shook her head. "No one threatened Blakeley, Mom. He was just walking and—" she gestured, groping for the most concise explanation possible "—you've heard the gossip. He's still recovering."

"Yes, I have heard. Bev Greenbriar says he's downright spooky and if it wasn't for the Regan fortune, he would be locked away in a you-know-what."

"I'd bet anything that big-mouthed Beverly hasn't been within a mile of Mead. For the record, he was extremely polite to me." Devan tried not to think about how she continued to feel his strong hand around her arm. "Let's look at the positive—Blakeley is fine and she learned a good lesson out of this."

"Yes, but—"

"It's over." Devan quickly hung her jacket and rushed to the cabinet where she stocked the aluminum foil. She was grateful Connie had been here to help, but she didn't want to discuss Mead with her another second. "Let me wrap some of this bread for you, and get you some lasagna. With all of your running for the sale, you'll be too tired to cook dinner for Dad."

Connie glanced at her watch. "Are you sure you have enough to spare? It does smell yummy."

"Thanks. No problem. I always make a full batch to portion and freeze anyway."

Devan continued her mindless chatting until she escorted Connie out the door and waved her down the street. Then she called to Blakeley, who she could hear had detoured from the bathroom to her bedroom—probably to delay that conversation that was promised.

As she waited for Blakeley, she glanced out the back door again. It was almost dusk. Had Mead made it back home? Was he all right?

The questions barely started in her mind before she thrust them away. She wouldn't let him turn her head again. The first time had cost her too much.

"I'm sorry for what's happened," she whispered against her clasped hands. "But stay away. Don't tempt me to care. I can't afford to care."

## Chapter Two

Mead didn't break any speed records returning home. He knew what awaited him there and slowed his pace to prepare for the inquisition, one that would be particularly grueling if the police had beat him there. He wasn't ungrateful for his mother's attention toward his recovery and understood she'd called in some serious IOUs to get him the best medical help beyond what the military had provided, which had been pretty damned fine from what he could tell. But what he craved was space in all of its ramifications. Since it was increasingly clear that he wasn't going to remember who he had been, he'd like to decide for himself who he wanted to be from here on. If he didn't grasp that before, that episode in the park with the little girl and her mother convinced him.

No doubt the poor kid had been scared. And her mother…Devan Anderson…who *was* that woman? It was nuts, but the moment she'd arrived, he'd felt as if the stream in the park had shifted ninety degrees and was suddenly carrying her energy straight to…no, *through* him. Whether she wanted to discuss it or not, he was convinced they had more of a history than she had admitted. Getting truthful answers would be the tricky part. It would happen, though, because until a few minutes ago, he hadn't been convinced that he belonged here, let alone figured out whom he wanted to gamble on trusting.

Spotting Pamela's majordomo at the back gate of the mansion, he steeled himself for the next step through his foggy maze. "Evening, Philo," he said to the compact man in the tailored gray suit. Pryce Philo's burr haircut was a duplicate of his except that it was completely silver and had him increasingly wondering if they didn't have more in common than easy-to-manage hair.

"Are you all right, sir?" the manservant asked in his polite, mid-Atlantic voice that gave away little of his background.

"You ask that a lot."

"Because Mrs. Regan expects regular and full reports, sir."

Mead paused outside the wrought-iron gate to study the man with the winter-cold eyes who had yet to release the lock. What did anyone know about Philo other than that he took as much pride in his appearance as he did his work, making him integral in keeping the estate running smoothly and its owner on schedule, if not out of trouble? Only Pamela and her CPA knew how valuable that was— and only she knew the full realm of his responsibilities.

"How long have you known me now, Philo?" It was a question he asked whenever he was totally frustrated with the puzzle and his environment and willing to push buttons, even if that meant shooting into the dark.

"I don't know you at all, sir," the manservant replied as usual. "But I've been privileged to be serving you on your mother's behalf for two weeks, two days…and almost a pair of shoes ago, Mr. Regan. It looks like you'll need a new pair yourself."

It was more than he and Philo usually had to say to each other, and Mead glanced down at his soggy athletic shoes and damp jeans to hide his smirk. Philo didn't like baby-sitting him any more than Mead cared for his salaried shadow. "Look at that."

"You might also like to know the police are here," Philo added. "They came to inquire about your whereabouts this afternoon."

"Did you sell me out?"

"You wound me, sir."

Mead didn't believe it for a minute. "I went for a walk beyond the sacred walls. Big deal."

"But there's the matter of a 911 call in the area. A child living on the other side of the park was feared—" Philo coughed discreetly "—attacked."

Tightening his fisted hands in his pockets, Mead replied coldly, "She wasn't. We ran into each other down there." He nodded in the direction of the park. "One look at me and she wanted her mommy or the marines—whichever she could find faster—and hightailed it home."

"Excellent. Allow me." Philo punched the security code into the keypad built into the wall and the gate lock opened with a subtle click. "Would now be a good time to ask how you managed to leave in the first place, since you don't have the code?"

"No." Mead stepped into the yard and waited for the sound of Philo closing up behind him.

"Have mercy, sir. Mrs. Regan is already in a state. In case you've forgotten, she's hosting another of her fund-raiser dinners this evening, and I think she and Mr. Walsh had something of a row earlier."

Mead had only observed Riley Walsh of Walsh Development and Construction, Inc.—his mother's choice as the next mayor of Mount Vance—from a distance, but even with his diminished abilities, his gut told him Pamela would be better off if the guy was dispatched to build ice condos in Antarctica.

"Sir?"

"If I tell you, will you let me slip upstairs and avoid your boss and the law?"

Pryce Philo laid his hand over his heart. "'A man cannot serve two masters.'"

"I bet you've tested that theory," Mead muttered. Shrugging, he gestured, "Lead on, faithful Philo."

One thing he couldn't deny as he returned to the house was that Regan Mansion, and its remaining twenty acres, was an impressive accomplishment. Having achieved centennial status, the three-story, Grecian-style mansion stood on what had been a massive pine and peach tree farm. Today it was a shutterbug's fantasy: acres of dogwood, red bud and azaleas in the spring, and magnolia mixed into the various pines in the summer. Was his mother's decision to sell off the land a good thing? Heaven knows, from the looks of things, she didn't need the money, but it was how the town had gotten the park. He'd gleaned that much information from one of the yard workers. Was it what the father he couldn't remember would have wanted? He suspected that was another question he would never get answered.

Mead followed Philo inside through the living room French doors and immediately heard his mother's second soprano voice resonating with anger all the way from the foyer.

"*Really,* Officer Brighton, I expect a formal apology from Chief Marrow. My son is a medaled war hero, was honorably discharged, and yet this is the manner with which he's welcomed home? Accusing him of such vile behavior?"

Cursing under his breath that his mother would use a messenger to vent her frustrations with Walsh—and him, too—Mead stepped into the foyer. "If you'd give the man a chance to hear his radio, I think you'll both learn that the situation is resolved."

In front of him he saw Pamela Niles Regan—his mother if documentation was to be believed—resplendent in a red, white and blue sequined jacket and an ankle-length, navy-blue skirt. The massive chandelier over her head accented the honey-gold highlights in her short, brunette coif, and her five-foot-three ripe body teetered on three-inch heels.

With a grateful glance, the flustered policeman keyed his shoulder mike. After a bit more static and some vague jargon Mead didn't understand, he heard the officer reply, "Copy."

To them the young man said with some chagrin, "It's confirmed. False alarm. Just doing my job, sir. Ma'am. Good evening to you."

As soon as the front door closed behind him, Pamela seethed, "Incompetent man. I'll have his badge."

"Don't." Mead slipped off his bandana, wearier from listening to those few moments of his mother's railing than from what happened earlier. "It was a misunderstanding. Let it go."

"Excuse me? Insult a national hero?"

"Stop it," Mead replied more tersely. "You don't know that."

Pamela lifted her chin. "Of course I do. They presented me with your ribbons and medals on your behalf. It's not my fault that you refuse to look at them."

Mead wrestled with a dark emotion he couldn't quite name. "The mission failed. People are dead. There's nothing to honor."

Once he'd gotten a fraction of his wits about him, he'd demanded someone tell him the truth. He couldn't confirm or deny anything said, but he didn't believe that he should have been rewarded for such pitiful results. Right now he wasn't sure he should believe he really was Mead Regan, or someone cosmetically altered to take his place. In the privacy of his bedroom, he'd looked for the telltale scars indicating plastic surgery and was almost disappointed to note that while he had scars, none were from that.

"The point is that you've repeatedly risked your life for your country, and this time almost lost everything. I nearly lost you." Pamela crossed to him and gripped his arm until perfectly manicured nails bit into the sleeve of his jacket. "You deserve respect and since you're too modest and noble to ask for it yourself, it's my job to see you get it."

Her saccharine smile turned into a grimace as she finally took notice of his appearance. "Good grief, Mead. I hope you haven't left a trail of mud on the carpet. Never mind, I'll have Philo look into that as soon as we finish. Now, I want you to go upstairs and shower. You can make up for giving me a fright by accompanying me at dinner tonight. Check the closet for your dress uniform. It might still be a bit loose on you, but it's been cleaned and you'll see I have all the medals on it."

Mead almost admired her. From day one after arriving here he'd noticed Pamela's steely determination. Her problem was that she directed it toward all the wrong things. Carefully disengaging himself, he replied, "No."

"No? Tonight is important to me."

"I thought this event was all about your buddy Walsh?"

Pamela's aging porcelain features hardened a second before she pressed her hands together and shifted her gaze over his shoulder. "Ah, Philo. Check the living room carpet for dirt, will you? And have the car ready at six."

"Very well, madam."

As the butler withdrew, Pamela refocused on Mead. "Darling...the fact of the matter is that I hate having to leave you yet again. I've had commitments so many times since your return, and we could use this as an opportunity to catch up. Besides, it's not good for you to be alone so much."

She was only now concluding that? "Last time I checked," Mead replied, "my birth certificate says I turn thirty-five in November. The head doctors wouldn't have authorized my release if I weren't relatively safe to be left on my own. For that matter, don't you think it's time to tell your watchdog that around-the-clock monitoring isn't necessary?"

"Philo has only made sure you didn't have an episode and had everything you need."

"The doctors told you I haven't since they changed my medication, and I've been off of all of it except aspirin for several days."

"That's wonderful. Then we can use tonight to celebrate." Pamela attempted a pout and coaxed, "I'd love to show you off to my friends."

He couldn't think of anything less appealing. "Did I ever enjoy performing for crowds?"

Stiffening, Pamela brushed past him and headed for the study. "I'm going to make myself a drink. Would you care for something?"

Mead's first impulse was to decline and seek refuge in his room, but on second thought he followed. He had more questions and, like it or not, she probably knew many if not all of the answers. "Beer sounds okay."

The tap of her high heels grew louder on the Italian tile. At the ornate antique huntboard that served as a bar, she filled two crystal glasses with ice from an open crystal bowl, then added a healthy splash of bourbon. "If I succeed at anything regarding your return," she said, handing him a glass, "it'll be to cure you of your pedestrian tastes."

Had his hunch that he'd always preferred beer to the expensive stuff been correct? Mead inspected the amber liquid. Contact with the person he'd been...

Pamela eyed him over her glass. "Oh, for heaven's sake, it's bourbon not tea leaves. Drink...and then tell me where you were to get in that condition."

He did sip...and with a frown put the glass back onto the huntboard. "Walking. Down by that creek behind this place. Who is Devan Anderson?" he added.

His mother stopped her glass inches from her lips. Her eyes narrowed, but not as though she was trying to remember.

"Who did you say?"

Mead recognized that he had made a mistake, and worried how bad. "The mother of the child who ran off. Surely Officer Brighton told you the little girl's name? Mrs. Anderson came into the park, too. She knew me."

Pamela took a second sip. "Everyone knows us."

There was no missing her pride, but that didn't help him one iota. His memory remained as void as his soul was troubled. Thinking became especially difficult in this museum of a house with its cathedral ceilings, furniture no one of size dared sit on without concern for their safety, and limited memorabilia to offer hints of any immediate family past. There wasn't so much as a photograph around, and the paintings were all of people in white wigs or breastplates.

"That doesn't answer my question." Mead knew his reluctance to address her as "Mother" irked Pamela, but in his opinion people earned titles as much as they did endearments. "Who is she?"

"Just a local." Pamela's sequined jacket glistened as she gestured with dismissal. "Dreamscapes Floral and Landscape Design. I use them on occasion. When their quotes are competitive."

"They? Is this a family business?"

"A partnership." Pamela rolled her eyes. "I suspect there were financial reasons to compel her to do it. Her husband Jay died over a year ago, and, no, I barely knew him except to figure out he wasn't exactly a rocket scientist. Anyway, by partnership, I mean Devan and that awful Lavender Smart. Lovechild of the sixties," she intoned with a look of distaste. "Devan must have a self-destructive streak in her as bad as yours."

Mead filed away the information—and Pamela's reaction—but decided not to push his luck by asking more. It was his inner reactions that intrigued him anyway. He didn't understand his strong curiosity…or was that attraction?

"I think I'll go lie down," he murmured, all but lost in his thoughts.

Pamela immediately transitioned into concerned mother. "What's wrong? Are you feeling ill?"

"No. I just want to—" He'd almost said "think." His mother would have pounced on that like she did new tidbits of gossip. "I must have overdone it walking."

"Are you sure? You do look drawn, now that you mention it. And I so wanted your company tonight." Pamela smiled bravely. "All right, darling, I'll manage on my own. You go rest. I'll give everyone your regrets."

Wondering who would care since he wasn't meant to attend in the first place, Mead climbed the stairs two at a time.

## Chapter Three

"Good night, dear. Be sure to bring Blakeley to our house for Halloween." Connie Anderson hugged Devan, planting an air kiss near her ear. "I'm making caramel apples."

Devan hoped her chuckle sounded sincere. "It's what she's been talking about since she recognized the date on the calendar. You keep spoiling her and I'll send you her dentist bills. Call you tomorrow. 'Night, Dad!"

With a wave to her pipe-smoking father-in-law standing in the background, Devan followed her daughter to the SUV and checked to make sure she got buckled in. Then she climbed behind the wheel, fastened her own belt and pulled away from her in-laws' home.

Although they'd just seen Connie yesterday, Devan did her best to have dinner with her and Jerrold at least once a week to keep the relationship between them and Jay's child alive and close. They were sweet—if rather staid—

people and it had been reassuring to be surrounded by their kindness and concern in the first months after Jay's death. She felt more blessed than she deserved to be. So why didn't the pressure in her chest ease until she was a block away from their house?

"Mom?"

"Blakeley?" They enjoyed that little tease to get each other's attention.

Grinning, Blakeley continued, "You think it would be okay to tell Nana that I like candied apples more than the caramel ones? D'you think she knows how to make them?"

"Ah, darlin', your daddy loved everything caramel. That's why she keeps up the tradition."

"What's tradition?"

For a moment Devan had the impulse to burst into song, namely the one from *Fiddler on the Roof*. She'd seen it at the Dallas Summer Musicals when she was a teenager. "Things people from one culture and era do that's unique to them. Like having turkey at Thanksgiving. Like having roast beast in Dr. Seuss's Whosville."

"Ooooh." After a considerable pause, Blakeley asked, "Then she must still love Daddy more than me."

Checking for nonexistent traffic, Devan eased the white Navigator through an intersection and passed the cemetery where her husband was buried. Mount Vance had a population under six thousand, and yet the cemetery was getting crowded. The balance of populations would get narrower if they didn't do more to keep people here and woo their young, educated people back to raise families. "Not getting your way isn't a sign of rejection, Blakeley," she said at last. "Daddy was her baby, the way you're mine. Her only one."

"Maybe I could remind her 'bout my favorite things?"

Devan ran her teeth over her lower lip, recognizing

shadows of her own youthful self-focus in her child. "No, sweetie, that's not a polite way to think. As we grow up, it's important to consider the feelings of others."

A sound of panic burst from Blakeley. "I could end up eating a lot of yucky stuff for a long time!"

The minx was going to make her burst out laughing yet. "Aw, c'mon. Doesn't it make you feel good when you see Nana's eyes sparkle down at you with pleasure when you say 'thank you' for something she worked on a long time? More than once I've surprised myself and tasted something I ended up really liking."

"Like what?"

"Oh...blue cheese dressing."

When all her daughter did was cover her face and moan, Devan did chuckle and added, "Okay. How about we share Nana's treat and get a candy apple for you from the bakery? I happen to have told them to reserve you one."

"Wow! *Thanks,* Mommy!"

Hoping that she wasn't setting herself up for an unexpected dentist visit, Devan made another turn, bringing them to Redbud Lane. But she delighted in her daughter's glee, for tonight had drained her more than family dinners generally did. Lately, as much as she respected her in-laws, they left her feeling increasingly stifled—as if she needed more of that in her life.

Since Jay's death sixteen months ago, people seemed to have narrowed down her existence to being Blakeley's mother and Jay's widow, and not much else. Even devoted and respectful customers of Dreamscapes often overlooked what it took to be a reliable entrepreneur in a town where two-thirds of the businesses were proprietorships or partnerships fighting to stay afloat, let alone out of bankruptcy court. How had this happened? And what was it doing to her personality? She used to be so independent and fearless. When everyone was sporting the Valley Girl look complete with big hair, she was into *Flashdance* fashion and cut her waist-length locks pixie short. When the uppity clique in school shunned a pregnant senior, Devan didn't just ruin her cheerleader chances by befriending her, she dumped her Jell-O into the squad captain's chicken noodle soup. Insignificant fluff compared to what was going on in the world today, but patterns were patterns.

Mead… All of this analysis was about seeing him again. Granted, she was grateful that he was alive, but she hadn't been happy to find herself face-to-face with her past. To realize that her child had been exposed to the unknown commodity he'd become had almost caused her an internal meltdown. Why hadn't he remained where she'd hidden him—deeply suppressed in her memories?

*Odds are he should be dead. Would that be better?*

Almost hiccuping as she pushed away those thoughts, Devan glanced into the rearview mirror. "Sweetie, are you sure there isn't anything we need to do before tomorrow?"

"No…the permission slip for the trip to the Christmas tree farm is in my backpack."

"Good. Then we can—" Blakeley's gasp silenced her.

"Who's that, Mommy?"

Beginning to turn into her driveway, Devan was slower than her daughter to see the person sitting on the front stoop; the porch light only gave her the benefit of identifying the person as male, an adult male, and yet fear never came into play. A sense of fatalism did. Somehow she knew from the first who it was. He had owned part of her mind since the instant she'd recognized him yesterday.

That didn't mean her heart didn't start pounding harder as adrenaline surged through her veins.

Knowing it would be only moments before Blakeley recognized him as the man from the park, Devan said quickly, "He's an old friend, sweetheart. The man in the woods? He's a soldier come home."

Blakeley said nothing.

A glance in the rearview mirror told Devan that her daughter was confused and apprehensive. Parking and shutting down the engine, she said gently, "Let's get you inside and you can watch a little TV, while I talk to Mr. Regan, okay?"

"Should I call 911?"

Devan swept her shoulder-length hair back as she realized this was no lightweight decision. "No, ma'am. When you get inside, change into your pj's, wash up and brush your teeth, and then you can see if there's something on your TV channels in my room. Okay?"

"No. But I guess."

Heaven help her, Devan didn't know what else to say to reassure her. Exiting the truck and slipping her purse strap over her shoulder, she circled around to Blakeley's door. Opening it, she stroked her daughter's cheek. "It will be fine. *Fine.* This man has never, ever, been unkind to me or to children, sweetie. Ever."

"Okay. Hurry, though."

Mead stood as they approached. He waited down on the lawn as she ushered her daughter inside. Blakeley kept her head down all the while, then ran to the back of the house as Devan shut off the alarm system and set down her purse. Then Devan stepped outside again and closed the door behind her.

When she joined Mead on the lawn, her confidence

wavered slightly. "Do you realize what it was like for her to see you sitting here?"

"I can't say I did before," he began, glancing at the door. "I do now. Sorry."

He was wearing the denim jacket and jeans again, but tonight the weather was milder and the jacket was open. She could see he had on a white T-shirt and noted that while she was right about him being thinner than she remembered, his body appeared toned. The lack of a bandana was the only other difference. Instead a clear Band-Aid covered his scar. Devan wondered about it. Was covering it for her or Blakeley's benefit? It had been a long time since he'd been hurt, so surely he didn't need a bandage anymore.

"What are you doing here?" she asked more kindly. "I'm surprised my neighbors haven't already notified the police that a stranger is lurking about."

Exhaling, he rubbed the back of his neck. "At the risk of upsetting you more, they're, um, not home."

She could have seen that if she had been more alert. Everyone on their block had full lives with most families including several children who were heavily involved in extracurricular activities. She bit her lower lip.

"I only came to apologize," Mead said wearily.

The simple, humble remark drew her focus back on him. But for Blakeley's sake if not her own, she had to remain cautious. "At this hour?"

"It's barely—" he glanced at his watch "—eight."

His confusion reminded her that even without his injury, he probably would know little to nothing of the kind of concerns and routines of young families. "Mead. As unfair as this may sound, these are difficult times, crime happens everywhere, even in small towns, and people can't be too careful. Especially not when children are involved."

"Yeah, I've been watching the news a lot. I don't know what it was like before, but it's sure a mess now. I should have realized how this would look." He grimaced and shoved his hands into his pockets. "I really am sorry, Devan. Everything is a learning experience for me these days."

That remark slipped straight through her defenses and touched her heart.

She couldn't begin to imagine what his ordeal was like. "How are you doing with that?" she asked slowly.

He uttered a brief, mirthless laugh. "I don't know. Compared to what?"

Devan saw a flash of vulnerability in him, and barely restrained frustration. Unwise as it was, the urge to reassure was instinctive and strong. "At least you're alive. Physically—" she gestured to encompass his tall form "—you're all there."

"Yeah, two hands, two feet, two eyes that work…if only we could locate my mind."

He sounded so sad Devan ached to go to him, to slip her arms around his waist and rest her head against his chest. She didn't dare, though, for so many reasons. Dear God, he could just have warned her that he wasn't to be trusted. "Do the doctors say, um, that you'll regain your memory someday? Any of it?" she added as his expression went from serious to grim.

"I've heard 'the brain is the least understood part of the body' so many times, I've stopped asking the doctors. Or keeping therapist appointments," he replied. "They're about as clueless as I am because I didn't just experience psychological trauma, I survived a head injury. As one surgeon put it without mincing words, my brain is going to let me know what and who it wants me to be. I can either go along for the ride, or opt out."

"'Opt out...'" Devan felt a cold finger race along her spine. No wonder there was such a haunted look in those dark eyes. He had to be constantly wondering—could he lose his mind rather than regain his memory or should he save himself prolonged torture by—she couldn't think the word let alone accept he would consider it. The thought of a world without him did exactly what she'd hoped to avoid, and she pressed her left hand against her heart. "Oh, Mead."

"Too much honesty, huh?" He shrugged. "Sorry. It's all I've got."

"You were always honest," she said gently.

She saw him look at her hand, realized he was looking at her ring. Self-conscious again, she quickly stuck her hand into her suede jacket's pocket.

"Was I? No one has told me that. Thank you."

Melting under his steady inspection, she tried to lighten the moment. "I'm not saying you were a saint—"

"Oh, my mother has pointed that out to me," he noted dryly.

"—But you never pretended to be anything you weren't."

"That's good to know."

His gaze roamed slowly over her face and his eyes warmed. He'd done that before, once relentlessly, and she couldn't help remembering what had followed.

"Can I ask you another question?"

Suddenly she felt like a minnow on a hook. "I guess."

"That baseball bat you had yesterday...do you play?"

She laughed, thinking self-deprecatingly, *That'll teach you.*

"No, it was Jay's. My husband's. He coached Little League when he wasn't busy taking over his parents' three dry-cleaning stores."

"He died."

Devan wondered how he knew? Had he asked Pamela? Of course, he must have; hadn't she told him to? "Yes. It was one of those freak things, an aneurysm.

"I'm sorry I can't say more, but I don't remember him."

"You didn't know him."

"Would I have liked him? I mean, could we have been friends?"

Although the five o'clock shadow that had made him appear more threatening yesterday was gone, Devan couldn't imagine two more different people. Jay had dressed in a tailored shirt and slacks no matter where he was except for the ballpark, and had shaved twice a day whether he needed to or not. He'd never missed church or Sunday dinner with his parents.

In contrast, Mead ignored social dictums and charmed his way out of faux pas. He had apologized to her once and smiled so beautifully, she suspected he wasn't being quite truthful. By his own admission, it had been years since he'd been to church, and while he was cited as a good soldier, she knew he had never been a diplomat. Add to that knowledge of what he wanted from a woman—and it wasn't compassion—she couldn't see them as having more than three words to say to each other except by accident.

"No, I doubt you would have been," she replied.

A flickering up the street caught her attention and she realized it was a flashlight. Of course, it was the usual time for Beverly Greenbrier to walk Jacque Blacque, her obnoxious standard poodle who had a rude fixation on the azalea bushes circling her mailbox and framing one side of the driveway. The second dose of emotional abuse was that Bev was a career gossip ranking right up there with Pamela Regan.

"Oh, God. Let's go inside," she said to Mead.

"What's wrong?" he asked, glancing around.

"A neighbor down the street is heading this way. She's too nosy not to stop and ply us both with questions, and she'll spend half of tomorrow on the phone sharing every word she gets out of us." Not waiting for him to reply, she led the way inside. Once in her living room, Devan gestured toward the kitchen. "Do you want a cup of coffee? I can make you a cup of coffee." Inwardly she groaned over her inane redundancy.

"I don't think that's a good idea," Mead replied, standing awkwardly in the middle of the room. "If it's okay with you, I'll just let myself out the back."

"You might want to wait a minute. She'll go around the corner and up the alley. I'm not kidding—she's as relentless as she is annoying."

"Maybe we should get away from all windows?"

He was teasing her, but she didn't mind that. She thought it was silly herself; however, he didn't understand the South and Southern women anymore.

"Huh. This is more like it."

She noticed he was looking around. "Pardon?"

"I like your house. I'm having trouble adjusting to my mother's."

"You said that before about the mansion…to her."

"Did I?"

"She was devastated."

"Somehow I doubt it."

Already cited as a monument to taste and quality, Pamela's house was a testament to the fortune she had spent after Mead Sr.'s death, trying to make it Texas's answer to the Biltmore Mansion. Glancing around, Devan was pleased that he approved of her far more modest home. No more than an eighth the size of the Regan mansion, the brick ranch was furnished with plush, inviting couches and chairs in sage and ivory. Across the room, a huge armoire encased the TV and stereo system. The cedar coffee table was large enough for someone to rest his feet on and still have room for assorted magazines, as well as Blakeley's coloring books and crayons. In the center a crystal bowl held the potpourri that filled the air with a fine pumpkin-cinnamon spice. It was only as she turned back to him that she realized Mead was studying the family photo of her, Jay and Blakeley on a side table.

"Your daughter favors you."

Devan thought so, too; they shared the same surprisingly abundant blond hair, same blue eyes and fair skin that somehow managed to tan easily in the summer. She was grateful, however, that her daughter had inherited her father's voice. Jay had been a soloist in the church choir. "Her name is Blakeley."

"How is she coping—and you, for that matter? I mean, without having her dad around."

"It's sad but no longer painful. And as strange as it might sound, I'm somewhat relieved for Blakeley because she was almost too young to remember him. We live close to Jay's parents, though, and that gives her a grandfather and a connection to the paternal side of her family."

"What about your parents?"

"My mother died the year I got engaged. My father hadn't been in our lives for a long time." He hadn't been the stick-to-it kind and had walked away from them before Devan turned thirteen. She was forgetting what he looked like, too, but there were times she felt his itch for adventure, for *passion*.

*That's the last thing you need to think about.*

She gestured to a chair. "Would you like to sit down?"

"I'd better not," he replied. "I may get too comfortable and forget that my mother is due home soon."

Devan couldn't help touching her fingers to her lips. "You couldn't sound less like yourself, Mead. It's… strange."

"Tell me about it."

"I guess it's ten times harder on you."

"No, I mean tell me about me. Us. What were we, Devan, really? I sense something."

What could she say? Confess that he'd been the man to jump-start her heart, that *he* had been the one—not her fiancé—to release that passion she'd been keeping locked tightly inside her? No, in this case, his lost memory was a blessing.

"It was a long time ago," she replied.

"Not that long. You're quite young and, at the risk of frightening you again, dare I say lovely. And despite what I see in the mirror, I'm not a total relic. How long could it have been?"

"I'd rather hear about you. What was recuperation like?"

"Six weeks in intensive care. Two—no, three operations. Another few months in the hospital. More in some clinic where people taught me what arms and legs were supposed to do, followed by even more time with a barrage of head doctors." Mead took a step closer to her. "What do you see when you look at me? Frankenstein's monster?"

Mesmerized by his voice as she was by his dark brown eyes, she admitted, "Hardly. But you look terribly sad… and you were never that. No Regrets Regan is how you referred to yourself."

"We were lovers."

His words held such conviction, Devan's throat locked trapping her with her own mixed emotions. "No," she rasped. She glanced down the hall, worried that Blakeley would hear some of this.

"The truth, Devan."

"Mead…it was one night."

"For some people that can be enough. If it's all they're given." He shook his head, his gaze once again moving over every inch of her face. "I wish I could remember. I've been trying every minute since yesterday. How did we part?"

"You went away. Exactly as you said you would."

"Did I say goodbye?"

Dear God, he was torturing her. "In a manner of speaking."

"Did I break your heart?"

"You couldn't, you never asked for it."

Mead's eyes narrowed. "I was going to come back to you."

The air left her lungs in a brief, mirthless laugh. "Ah…no. Promises and commitment weren't for you."

"Then I was an ass."

In her weakest moments, Devan had imagined having this conversation. But that was restricted to late at night, on the worst nights when she lay alone and lonely in her bed; when her memories refused to let her sleep and her body ached with the need for someone as hungry as she.

As she saw curiosity become desire in Mead's eyes, she realized he had seen that…and was going to kiss her. *Yes,* her soul whispered.

Just as he started to reach for her, someone knocked at the storm door. Startled back to reality, Devan launched herself across the room. Her heart pounded anew as she recognized Officer Billy Denny on the front stoop.

"Mrs. Anderson," he said as she opened the door. His gaze shifted to Mead. "Everything all right?"

"Why, yes, Officer Denny. Is there a problem?"

"Well, your neighbor saw a stranger outside of your house and when she saw him follow you inside, she was concerned you were in danger. She'd heard about the trouble in the park."

Devan glanced around him and saw Bev Greenbriar stretching to see what was going on. The old busybody, she fumed to herself; she knew perfectly well who Mead was, and by morning this was going to be all over town.

"That's very kind of her," she said with a forced smile. "But as you can see, everything is fine. Mr. Regan was just apologizing again for yesterday and checking to see if Blakeley is okay."

"Fine. Would you like a lift home, sir?" the young cop asked. "I'd feel better if you'd allow me. We had a rabies incident today, and you'd best not take any chances that some infected critter might cross your path or something in the park."

"I'd appreciate it," Mead replied. At the door, he met Devan's apprehensive gaze. "Thanks for being so understanding."

"It was good of you to stop by," she said with equal formality.

As soon as he was outside and he and Officer Denny were heading to the car, Devan locked the storm door and shut and locked the inner one. She didn't want to take any chance that Bev would have the nerve to charge up here to fish more information out of her, while rude Jacque defiled their pumpkin display.

But as she leaned back against hardwood, she knew that wasn't why her heart was pounding, or why her face was feverishly hot.

Touching her fingertips to her lips she closed her eyes. What had she almost done?

*Exactly what she'd promised herself she would never do again.*

## Chapter Four

"I promise, Laureen, I'll talk to him about starting his motorcycle under your bedroom window and waking you and the birds." Lavender rolled her eyes as Devan entered Dreamscapes. "Okay. I've got customers, hon, gotta go now. Make love not war. 'Byee."

Hanging up the phone, thirty-four-year-old Lavender Smart swept her wild mane of flaming red hair and purple extensions from her face and noisily purged the air from her lungs. "Is it happy hour yet?"

Devan gave her a droll look as she shifted the thigh-high rabbit yard ornament by the door to keep it open. "Please. Not only is it barely past eight in the morning, but half this town is Baptist. Keep it down." However, she'd recognized the name of her partner's neighbor, Laureen Moyers. "Is Rhys in trouble again?"

"Heck, yeah. How can she complain about having a

cop right next door adding to her personal security?" Lavender finished tying a green Dreamscapes apron over her jeans and favorite kitten T-shirt with the slogan, I Am Leo, Hear Me Roar.

"Oh, I imagine it has something to do with your active love life and her comatose one." Devan recalled that fifty-something-year-old Mrs. Moyers was a widow three times over and only months after moving in and getting to know her highly critical neighbor, Lavender had had the poor judgment to suggest to her that each spouse had seen their demise as the preferred escape from the woman. Ever since that Laureen had taken exception to whomever Lavender invited to share her bed with…and there had been several invitees. To Lavender the opposite sex was like a candy store: too many choices to settle on just one.

"Well, she better get over it. Is it his fault that he's on the early shift?"

Passing a display of gifts, Devan shifted a ceramic box adorned with pansies that looked too close to the edge of the table. "You don't think he's pushing her buttons?"

"Of course he is 'cuz he's caught her peeking into the bathroom window whenever he's showering, and in the kitchen window when he's grabbing a beer after we've given the mattress a little workout. Mr. Cute Butt just figures she wants to get another look at him as he heads to the station."

Never knowing what will come out of Lavender's mouth, Devan gnawed on her cheek to keep from bursting into laughter. "It sounds like you and Mount Vance's newest uniform are made for each other."

"Now don't go getting ideas. He's closer to your age, not mine. Heck, I'll be menopausal like that rottweiler next door and Rhys Atwood will still look like a *Playgirl* centerfold." Lavender fanned herself with her hand. "Oh, help. I'm thinking myself into a hot flash already."

Devan gave up and giggled as she rounded the counter and patted her friend's back. "I swear it would take a naval fleet for you to suffer seximus maximus, Lav."

"Ho-ho, you're one to tease, guess who called before Laureen asking about a certain somebody being at your house last night? Yvonne Ledbetter. Now tell me, Ms. Look Not Want Not, *what* on earth made you cut the steel corset and finally open your door to a man—Mead Regan no less?"

Devan had made it to the closet where she and Lavender put their purses, personal things, and kept the safe. She'd just come from dropping off Blakeley at day care and was only ten or twelve minutes late. She couldn't believe so much had happened already. "So Beverly Big Mouth's speed dial finger strikes again. Incredible. I knew she'd be spreading gossip, but I never thought she would call Yvonne Ledbetter." Yvonne was Bev's ex-sister-in-law. Although that marriage ended fifteen years ago, they would as soon toss each other's car keys in a public commode than be the first to suggest bygones be bygones.

"Ah," Lavender countered. "But Yvonne's Charlie is city manager and you said yourself that Mrs. Regan's car is parked outside of city hall more often than the mayor's. My guess is that Bev couldn't resist tempting Yvonne to be the first to pass on the news seeing as I'm your partner and she keeps my mane so marvelous."

Locking the door again, Devan considered all that could trigger, but the machinations were too much for her tired mind. "There are more dysfunctional people in this town," she fumed under her breath.

"Don't make me one of 'em." Lavender leaned a generous hip against the counter. "Tell me what's going on."

Devan owed her friend and business partner an explanation but could only bring herself to share the official version. The full story was too private, as was her history with Mead.

Even so, Lavender's hazel eyes were twinkling. "I should rename you Sleeping Beauty. You get more male attention saying 'get gone' than most of the single girls in this town do primping and preening. If I wasn't financially bound to you like an umbilical cord, I'd hate you."

Which was one of the reasons Devan and Lavender got along so fabulously. There wasn't an ounce of envy between them, and sharing the same birth month, they understood each other like twins, even though they seemed to be personality opposites. "When you run out of gush, let me know," Devan said with a tolerant smile. Inside, however, she was worrying about how Pamela Regan was going to take this.

Lavender snatched up two faxed orders from the tray. "I'm done because I really should be mad at you. Why didn't you call and tell me he showed up again?"

"I had to get Blakeley into bed, get a load of laundry in the washer, pay some bills. And I was already exhausted."

"Okay, but you let him *into* your house? Didn't you feel a bit uncertain? I mean, the man was trained to kill people, probably has killed people."

Devan couldn't help wincing. "Lav, he was a soldier, what do you expect?"

"And now he's a human time bomb, what with the lost mind and everything."

"Memory! He's lost his memory, not his mind."

"Well, Bev said he's on drugs they give psychotics or something."

"When did Beverly Greenbriar meet Mead and get that information? And I can't recall her being a friend of Pamela's."

"Then tell me. What's he like now? I saw a photo of him in the paper and he looks kind of gray and grim."

Devan kept her gaze on the clipboard she'd retrieved from under the counter that contained today's job sheets. "You would, too, if you'd gone through what he has. He's a quieter man now, and thoughtful. He was very kind and concerned about Blakeley. And for the record, he looked much better than the day before."

"Did he now?"

Hearing the note of speculation entering her friend's voice, Devan knew it was time to run. "I'm getting the guys and going to work."

"Wait—I've got an order for an orchid basket. Will you pick out a pot for me while I go choose a plant? You seem to understand those things so much better than I do. I swear those and African violets are killers for me."

"Sure. Go. Just tell the guys to finish scarfing down the sausage and biscuits you brought them this morning," she added, referring to Jorges Luna and the other four young boys they hired for various jobs.

"I know, I know. I'm corrupting them, but the younger ones are so far from home, and look so lonely at times. Back in five."

Devan shook her head as Lavender dashed through the French doors to the nursery and hothouse beyond. She had earned her spread-the-love attitude honestly from her flower child parents who these days ran an organic vegetable farm in Oregon. An older brother painted set scenery on Broadway—when he wasn't honing his mime technique at Central Park—and a younger sister worked at a private animal rescue farm in California.

Relieved they'd cleared the subject of Mead, Devan got herself a last cup of coffee from the machine in the workroom and checked their computer to see what else was pending for today. Lavender had already posted three orders for Mrs. Enid Coe at the workstation table. Poor soul was eighty-something and had been a good customer, often scouring the greenhouse looking for African violets and roses out in the nursery. What a shame to think she was in the hospital yet again.

Wanting to send something herself, she was back at the counter filling out an order sheet, and was slow to notice that the shadow falling over the counter was a person and not moving limbs from the trees across the street in the square.

"Hi, can I help—" she blinked "—you."

Mead stood on the other side of the counter looking tall, freshly shaved and more respectably dressed in a white dress shirt, pressed jeans and a blue windbreaker. "Morning," he said.

As if that wasn't surprise enough, out of the corner of her eyes she noticed movement and to her consternation realized two of the morning park bench sitters were on their feet and leaning over their canes and walkers to peer from across the street at them. Closer yet was Judy Melrose from Melrose Insurance next door, who had stopped at the far end of the display window, mostly hidden by the life-size scarecrow, to stare at Mead.

"How did you get here?" Devan didn't see a car out front—she didn't know if Mead could even drive yet. "I mean, it's so early."

"The sign says you open at eight."

"True." Accepting that she was acting like a fool, she took a stabilizing breath and smiled her welcome. "What can I do for you?"

He glanced toward the display cooler. "I wanted to place an order. But that's a lot of flowers to choose from."

Devan considered that a compliment. "We're fortunate to still be the only florist in town and that brings us considerable business from the outer areas of the county." Struggling to ignore the commotion as Judy was joined by one of her office staff, Devan added, "Did you have something in mind? A certain flower, style, price range?"

He remained silent for several more seconds before asking, "What would you choose?"

She and Lavender were often asked for their advice—or were left to their own discrimination. "It all depends on the occasion and what you're trying to say." She grew hesitant. "This isn't for a funeral, is it? You didn't get a bad phone call last night? Your mother didn't get ill on another rubber chicken dinner?"

"Well, she did eat out, but all seems okay so far."

Clearing her throat, Devan tried to restrain an outright grin. "Then this is a birthday, anniversary, thank you or…just because gift?"

"Is it possible to…blend the latter two?"

"Sure, and how nice." It was good to see him again and Devan hoped this meant his mother wasn't upset that he'd stopped by last night. Or was this some last gesture before the ax fell? "That leaves you with lots of choices, in fact just about anything will work aside from calla lilies—although, personally, I adore them for elegant evening centerpieces."

"You do?"

"Aside from just loving white flowers, they're graceful yet surprisingly sturdy." She gestured toward the long-stemmed beauties in the lower bucket. "If you're sending these to a lady, white embodies everything—beauty, spirituality, nature at her most gentle. Whatever the flower—gladiola, carnation, rose—okay daisy is a bit impish—but the rest are saying a dozen things with each blossom via their purity." Remembering that Lavender would be back in a moment, she cleared her throat and resumed her hastier sales pitch. "But those yellow roses are particularly vibrant this week, and so are the coral ones. On the other hand, we can do a sparkling bouquet with multiple seasonal colors. Your choice—I promise Dreamscapes never disappoints."

Mead studied the cooler once again. "I guess the white roses are the way to go."

Pleasure warred with regret as Devan reached for the order pad. She'd loved looking at them since they arrived yesterday afternoon and hoped whoever received them would appreciate how special they were—as was the person taking such care in choosing them. As she filled in his name, she said, "Lucky whomever. Okay, how many?"

"All of them."

A muted cough drew Devan's attention outside again. In the doorway stood Barry Sweat, Precinct 2 Constable in Franklin County. The one and only time he'd been into the shop had been to buy three carnations for his third wife for Valentine's Day. Devan wanted to go out and suggest he pay more attention to the potholes over by their neighborhood than to eavesdropping. Instead she leaned across the counter to keep her voice low. "Mead, there are three dozen."

"That's what I figure."

She didn't doubt he could afford them but didn't want to be seen as taking advantage. On the other hand, the sooner she got this over with, the sooner she would stop being the morning entertainment. "Just checking. Do you want us to bill you? Your mother has an account."

Mead pulled out his wallet. "I'll take care of it."

Expecting a credit card, Devan was surprised to see him pull out cash. "Fine. Now where do we deliver?"

"Three twenty-seven Circle."

The seven ended up looking like one of those tin curlicue wind-catchers, and for good reason. The address was hers. Almost. Looking up, she met his calm scrutiny. "Do you mean Lane?"

"Is it Lane? Lane."

"What are you doing?" she demanded, not believing this was happening.

The carousel of sentiment cards stood on the counter and he turned it, studying the offerings. "Can I choose and write my own?"

"No. Yes. I mean…Mead, you can't come in here and— send me flowers."

"Where else should I go?"

"Nowhere. There's no reason to do this. No need." Through the French doors she saw Lavender heading back. How her friend would eat this up. A born romantic as well as an optimist, Lavender had come into town almost three years ago with her then boyfriend in a beaten-up van. The boyfriend and van had moved on, but she had stayed. Seeing Devan "matched up better" was always on her mind. "Please, Mead. It's a lovely gesture, but no."

He studied her and some light dimmed in his eyes. "You're embarrassed that I'm here."

*"No."* Impulsively, Devan put her hand over his. "It's not that simple—and hopefully, I'm not that shallow. But this enterprise isn't just about me. I have a partner and we have debt. There are customers we can't afford to lose."

"My mother."

"Among others."

"Riley Walsh?"

"It would be unethical for me to say anything else."

"Let me worry about my mother," he said, nodding to the pad. "Take the order or I'll figure some other way to do this."

Why? Did he even know? No, he seemed stable enough; she wouldn't listen to gossip. But even so, fear gripped her. Was this incredible gesture the sign that he intended to continue with the mind-set that he'd broached last night? She couldn't let him. On the other hand, losing the sale and explaining the reason to Lavender would be no party, either.

Devan decided to total his bill, then she took the cash to make change. "Thank you." She kept her eyes on what she was doing. "Really. This is…lovely."

"You're welcome. When can I see you again?"

He was going to scrape her insides raw. "Mead, I'm so shaken, I'm about to lose the breakfast I barely ate."

Confusion shadowed those dark eyes. "I've made you sick?"

"Oh, no! It's because—" how did she make him understand? "—I did an extra good job convincing myself that I'd never see you again. And then there's the man you were. I don't believe he…you would be doing this."

"But *I* am." He leaned closer to force her to meet his gaze. "Would you be hoping I would?"

She couldn't bring herself to answer.

That won a real smile from Mead and he dropped the bulk of the cash she'd returned to him onto her copy of the invoice. "Add the yellow roses."

"Oh, no, Mead, please—"

"Think about me, not who you think I should be, or the people you keep looking at outside. Not my mother."

As he left, Lavender burst through the French doors with her usual energy and curiosity. "Who was *that*? Whoa—long legs, tight butt and shoulders so wide he wouldn't notice if I ate a pint of ice cream every night. Did he place an order?"

"Does the word Rhys ring a bell with you?" Devan said, a little exasperated.

"Of course." Lavender set a glorious purple orchid on the counter. "I'm just asking."

"Yes, he placed an order."

"Super, so we've got his phone number."

"We already have it on file."

"We do?

"It's the same as Pamela Regan's."

"Oh. *Oh...*wow."

Devan sighed. "You can say that again."

## Chapter Five

It was a relief that Dreamscapes' business increased by the day to help keep Devan preoccupied. While Lavender continued to tend to the floral orders, she and her team were forced to spread themselves thin to fulfill all of the requests to create holiday porches and scenescapes, and still finish landscaping yards for Riley Walsh's new houses. That entailed longer hours and, as a result, the necessity to take up the Andersons' offer to pick up Blakeley from day care and feed her dinner. Yesterday had been so grueling she even had to let them keep her overnight; it was healthier and kinder to let the child stay warm and get good rest than to drag her in and out of the SUV in the damp, chilly night air.

Today, however, they'd managed to finish in time for Devan to spend the evening with her child. Nevertheless, it was all she could do to get Blakeley bathed and tuck her into bed before feeling ready to collapse, too.

"'Night, sweetheart."

"You didn't read me a story, Mommy. Nana has been reading me a story every time."

"So do I, remember? But Mommy's throat is a little raw tonight."

"Are you catching a cold from chasing the all mighty?"

Her hand on the light switch, Devan paused. "What?"

"Gramps told Nana that's what you've been doing. He said that it would be better if you stayed home and didn't chase it. All mighty what, Mommy? I heard that name in Sunday school, but that was God. I thought God was in heaven. Did he move to Mount Vance?"

Did she need this? Devan wondered. She certainly didn't feel she deserved such a remark behind her back. It didn't surprise her, though. Connie was quite good about accepting that their generation's lifestyles were different than today's. Or at least she didn't force her opinion on people. For some reason Jerrold seemed obliged to protect his son's memory, maybe males in general, and he didn't care for her to be a businesswoman.

It was true that Jay had been a good provider and hard worker. The profit from selling the three dry-cleaning stores had been safely invested to guarantee Blakeley her future. His life insurance had paid off the mortgage on the house and still could take care of them on a day-to-day basis, too. But what about her? Didn't she deserve to challenge herself and pursue goals?

Sighing, she smiled at Blakeley and gave her a last kiss before turning off the light. "Gramps was just sharing an opinion with Nana. He didn't mean for you to hear."

"Because it's secret stuff? He didn't whisper."

Devan bet he didn't. "No, boring grown up stuff about work. Sweet dreams, darlin'."

Returning to the kitchen to load the dishwasher, tears burned in her eyes, and that wasn't because virtually every muscle in her body screamed with fatigue. Afraid she was going to burst into tears, she buried her face in her hands.

She couldn't let what Blakeley told her pull her down. Mind-sets like Jerrold's were steeped in generations of Southern living. It didn't mean he disapproved of her or had been pretending to care about her all this time.

*You've got to be hormonal.*

Knowing that as tired as she was, she would just lie there and watch the numbers on her digital clock change, she poured herself a glass of Shiraz, switched off the TV, and put on a CD of New Age music Lavender had asked her to listen to. They were considering carrying some romantic CDs to offer in their gift baskets and arrangements.

By the stereo was one of the vases with the white roses Mead had insisted on giving her the other day. There were vases in both her bedroom and Blakeley's as well as on the dining room table, and their scent continued to fill the house and stir her emotions. She couldn't get over what he'd done, or stop staring at the blossoms wondering why life was taking this latest twist.

Two years ago this would be the time of night when Jay would flip the TV remote through the financial shows, then the sports channels while she would polish the kitchen whether it needed it or not. Afterward, she would soak in the tub with a steamy novel that soon had her aching and wishing he wasn't such a robot about their relationship. Their marriage hadn't been a failure—there was an easiness, a tenderness that others said they'd envied—but she couldn't deny that sometimes she was bored to desperation with its predictability.

Well, she thought yet again, who said life was supposed to be the Fourth of July every day?

*How about one night a month? At least one night a year?*

She knew uncontrollable passion existed. Sweet heaven, did she.

Heat rose in Devan like a furnace switched to full blast. She took a sip of wine, pulled one of the roses out of the vase and slipped out the back door to cool off. It was either that or ditch the wisteria-blue tunic-sweater she wore over a white turtleneck.

The porch light was off, but the rising moon illuminated the yard adequately for the minute or two she would be out here. Her rose looked all the more magical in that light and she stroked the velvety petals against her cheek.

Tomorrow she needed to remember to ask Lavender if she wanted to dry the petals for potpourri. Taught by her mother, Lavender was gaining a following for her experimentation of unusual scents. Devan had forgotten to ask her this evening due to a last-minute phone call from Pamela Regan demanding yet another change for the Chamber banquet on Saturday. Pamela didn't bring up Mead, the episode in the woods, anything, but Devan didn't doubt she knew and was continuing to harvest information on her and any additional meetings with her son better than any U.S. intelligence agency.

*Oh, Regans, get out of my head!*

As though to mock that thought, a shadow separated itself from the woods and sprang across the fence. Devan's breath locked in her throat. But just as she was about to dash back inside and bolt the door, she recognized the intruder's stride, the breadth of his shoulders and the way he hunkered into the upturned collar of his jacket.

"I wondered if I could will you outside," he said once

he got near enough where a murmur could be heard. "I was watching you through the window."

For how long? She didn't want to think about it. Thank goodness her hands were full, though, to keep her from exposing her self-consciousness and touching her messy ponytail. This evening she'd been so drained she hadn't combed it out before dinner as she usually did.

"Mead...you shouldn't be here."

"Your neighbor went by when you put Blakeley to bed. Her dog picked up my scent and growled. She got so scared she didn't bother turning her flashlight beam on me, she just rushed the rest of the way down the alley." He sounded amused.

"Don't you realize if she had spotted you, you would seem like the stalker she suggested?" Weak-kneed, she lowered herself onto the flat bench against the garage wall.

"It's turning out to be my favorite time of day to walk. Could be more of that training I can't remember." He shrugged. "Anyway, it beats being stared at."

That was anything but reassuring. Devan had the option to either think of his life as a commando, or wonder if rumor was right that his injuries had left him a walking time bomb.

"Don't brood over it," he added when she failed to reply. "You're upset enough. What's wrong?"

She made a small negative movement with her head. "Nothing worth repeating. A small family thing."

Mead sat on the knee-high patio wall between pots of chrysanthemums. "You're a slightly built woman, Devan. Resilient, no doubt, but finely made. And I don't need a memory to recognize that you have a lot on your plate. My returning here seems to have added to that."

"This is your home. You have a right to be here."

He looked away. Despite the soft light, his profile was stone-hard and grim. "I don't know about that. I'm not sure I want to stay. Being here is like being in a virtual joke, except that everyone but me knows the punch line—and it *is* me."

"Oh, Mead."

He shrugged again. "It's appealing in a way, the idea of leaving. At least whoever I met would be as clueless about me as I am about them."

"Your mother would be devastated." In truth, Devan didn't entirely believe that, but it was a way to avoid acknowledging how her own insides were plummeting and she feared the rest of her would cave in on the resulting emptiness.

Mead responded with a low sound of scorn. "Come on, Devan, one thing I recognize about Pamela is that she's a survivor. I have a feeling the only reason she had me was to give my father an heir."

"Now you sound like a soldier."

"As in cold-blooded?"

"Pragmatic."

"Was I that way before?"

She was the wrong person to ask. "I didn't see you every day, so I can't judge fairly. You're five years older than me, too, and that put you way ahead in school."

"My mother made sure the yearbooks in my room are open to strategic pages." He rested his elbows on his knees to allow him to be closer. "I looked for you in them, but couldn't find you."

"I started Mount Vance High the year you left for college."

"So when did we meet?"

"Rather, when did you finally notice me?"

His gaze caressed her. "You're a beautiful woman, Devan. I figure I noticed from the moment you hit puberty."

"Not with the likes of Megan Maples, Darcie Tracy, Carly Ferris and others competing for your attention."

An involuntary chuckle burst from his lips and Mead self-consciously rubbed his jaw. "My mother put sticky notes by Megan's and Darcy's names. She wrote that Megan is the daughter of the bank president, and the bank remains independently owned and has three branches in neighboring communities, while by Darcy's name there's just one word—oil. Oh, and she also noted they were both single."

Devan wasn't surprised at Pamela's not-so-subtle assistance in helping Mead with his memory. Pedigree was all-important to her, as it was to many Southerners. "Who are your people?" and "What church do you attend?" were common and acceptable icebreakers when welcoming a newcomer to a community that continued to embrace old Southern traditions.

"What she left out is that they're accomplished women," she replied. "Meg owns the most successful real estate firm in the county. Darcie happens to be an attorney in her father's oil company."

"Why do you suppose she left out Carly?" Mead asked.

"Carly's fortune is inherited and she recently buried her second husband. Stunning though she is, you may be too young for her tastes."

This time Mead threw back his head and laughed out loud. "Well, I can't begin to think of what we'd talk about now."

Too aware of Pamela's determination, Devan could only smile. "It was good to see you laugh anyway."

"Don't think I didn't notice you changing the subject away from you."

In an attempt to keep things light, she quipped, "Ah, but we were discussing your long list of conquests."

He didn't even smile this time. "Was I a skirt-chasing SOB, Devan? Is that why you kept me at arm's length, as you apparently did...and are trying to do again?"

She didn't use such expressions, even on people who clearly deserved them, and it was painful to hear he worried he could be one of those. "You were never that. You could seem aloof, but that's because you never wasted time suffering fools, and when a girl failed to get a proposal out of you, they sometimes stroked their injured pride by announcing that you were emotionally cold and that ending the relationship was their idea. You remained a gentleman, graciously never contradicting them."

His chest rose and fell on a deep breath. "Talk about being gracious...you really did understand me, didn't you? Is that what I felt when we met again? It was like nothing else I've experienced since waking in that hospital bed."

Devan had to put down her glass for fear of him seeing how his comment left her hands shaking. The one holding the rose she rested in her lap. "Mead, a lot of people understood you, you just haven't been exposed to them yet. You didn't lack for friends or attention."

"My father's fortune could explain that."

No one except the most naive could deny that possibility for some, but Devan couldn't let him miss something important. "You loved life, and that enhanced your natural charisma. You were always seeking something, eager for experience. At least, that was my impression," she quickly concluded, suddenly embarrassed. What nerve she'd had accusing Lavender of gushing the other day. With her motor mouth, she would yet expose that she hadn't just watched him from afar, she'd studied him with rapt fascination every chance she'd had.

"Hmm," Mead murmured, his expression skeptical. "Is this where you break the bad news that this search for experience got me into a lot of fights? It sure would explain how I got into the work I did."

"You never started a fight that I know of, and stopped at least one that I saw." Devan sighed. "Mount Vance was just too small for you. The days of sailing off to sea to find one's own fortune and honor are over. You did the next best thing for you."

"I'm sorry."

"What for? Thinking Mount Vance was stifling you? There was a time I agreed with you." She hadn't planned on confessing that, and to her dismay he latched on fast.

"So why did you stay?"

That was a long story, and a much more boring one than his. "Narrower options," she said with a dismissive shrug.

"Were you able to continue with school?"

"The community junior college." That was where she really got to know Jay, even though he'd been only a year ahead of her in high school. Somehow he'd never caught her attention sooner. There was no reason for her to examine why.

"When did we get to know one another?"

"We didn't. I told you the truth, Mead. We weren't friends." She could see by his expression, however, that he wasn't convinced. "You began noticing me during your trips home on leave. It was flattering, believe me, but I was still a kid and you had plenty of options without dipping into the jailbait barrel."

"We must've talked. I told you, I haven't experienced this connection with anyone else. That can't be something out of the blue."

"Oh, I think it happens." At least in books, movies and

her fantasies. "Okay, the fact is, one of my part-time jobs to pay my way through school was at the Dairy Queen and you'd come breezing through the drive-thru with your flavor of the weekend. I kinda got a reputation with you for giving you a bit of a hard time."

He raised his eyebrows a second before his firm mouth curled appreciatively. "At the risk of sounding full of myself, did you just sound almost jealous?"

It was all Devan could do not to reach for and swallow the rest of her wine. Glancing up at the sky, she groaned. "That was worse than catty, that was juvenile."

Mead reached over to place a hand on her knee. "It was adorable. And obviously, you were right on instinct-wise to give me heck. None of those ladies has tried to contact me, and I sure would know if they'd talked to my mother. I suspect the charisma was blown to hell along with some of the gray matter."

"You're being too hard on yourself."

He grew still to where he appeared to stop breathing. "You come to my defense so quickly for someone who doesn't want to be seen with me."

Devan didn't know how many of these blows to her solar plexus she could take. "Not want—how can you say that?" she gasped, rising to escape his touch.

"If I asked you out, what would you say?"

Her fingers tightened around the rose stem and the whole thing trembled as she held it toward him. "Is that why you did this? To oblige me into having to say yes?"

"Would it work?"

"It's time for you to go home, Mead."

He rose, but made no attempt to leave. "I'd like an answer to my question."

"All right then...no," she said shakily. "Because strange

as it might sound, my instincts are to protect you as much as myself."

Bemused, he replied, "Let me take care of me."

"You who don't even know if you are you," she cried, "never mind comprehending that I could be your worst enemy."

Smiling now, Mead shook his head. "Devan, if you're going to talk crazy sweet like that, I'll have to kiss you."

"Ouch!" The rose fell out of her grasp as she gripped her left hand with her right.

Mead immediately reached for her, too. "What happened?"

She backed into the wall, trying to avoid his touch. "It's stupid...just a thorn scratch."

"Let me see."

"I'll take care of it. Please, Mead, tomorrow is going to be another killer day and I need to—"

Ignoring her, he brushed away her right hand and opened her fist to peer at the wound. "It's bleeding, but in this dark, I can't see if the thorn is imbedded."

Before she could repeat her promise to see to it herself, Mead bent and closed his lips over the inside of her ring finger. His ministrations were tender, yet the heat they exuded gave no relief. How could they when she could feel his tongue against her wedding band, against her skin? Her throat, already sore, burned as though it was drying into sandpaper while the rest of her body liquefied into quicksilver.

"I'm sorry," he murmured when he raised his head.

"Really, it's nothing. If I don't end up with a cut or bleeding blister at least once a week, my crew thinks there's been Divine Intervention."

He just stared at her. "Don't. Don't try to turn this into a joke. Do you know what the moon does to your lovely eyes? It makes them even clearer…even more honest. I can see straight to your soul, Devan. You can't hide from me."

He released her hand, only to frame her face. Devan's heart threatened to burst through her sternum. "Mead, I'm glad you're alive. But I wish…oh, God, I'm sorry, but I wish you'd never come back."

"I did, too. Until now."

Lowering his head, he gently brushed his lips across her cheek, kissed her brow, the corner of her eye, then nipped the tender skin just below her right ear. When that released a shaky breath from her, he stepped even closer until the full length of his body was only a stitch away from hers. Then he traced another series of whispery kisses along her throat, across her face, coming closer and closer to her lips. She wanted him there. The craving was growing so strong, she ached with it.

"Patience," he whispered. "Someone came to the hospital once. I was delirious and blind with pain. He kept repeating, 'In patience possess ye your soul.' I think I'm about to understand."

Transfixed by his words, as much as his caresses, Devan rasped, "Did you…did you find out who?"

"No. As I got better, I kept listening for that voice again whenever someone came into my room. I never heard it."

"A miracle?"

He paused, his gaze locked on her lips with rapt fascination. "I didn't believe in them before. I think I may have to change my mind." Then slowly, slowly, just as a whimper of desire rose in her throat, he opened his mouth over hers and absorbed the sound as he did her essence.

Devan surrendered to the moment and him. There was no use pretending she didn't want this. She'd been yearning to feel this exhilaration for more than sixteen months, maybe even six years, although she couldn't bring herself to consider that yet. But the instant his tongue stroked hers in a silent invitation to join him in this intimate dance, she yielded and responded, until with a low moan, he angled his head the other way to get more.

That still wasn't enough and soon he shifted his hands to place them flat against the wall and molded the rest of his body to hers as perfectly as he had their mouths. The electricity that left him shuddering raced into her.

It was like being swept up into the vortex of a storm, and all Devan could do was rise on tiptoe, wrap her arms around his neck and pray, pray he didn't stop, pray he didn't let her fall to earth and reality. She knew if he did, at least a part of her would be dead forever. She'd believed it already was, but his coming back showed her how wrong she was.

Devan felt his heart thrum, his arousal stir against her. That triggered flashbacks of a perfect night, how he had repeatedly moved inside her, and spontaneously had her arching her hips in response.

"Devan…" Her name was a prayer, then an oath, as Mead slid his hands down her body, brushing over the outer swell of her breasts, her waist…downward until he relearned the delicious shape of her firm bottom. Tightening his hands, he lifted her higher and harder against him, rocking to match the rhythm of their kiss.

Their shallow breaths blocked out the faint stereo music, and Devan's mews and Mead's moans had the same effect on the night sounds. In her mind, she saw them by her bed, Mead breaking the kiss only to cover her bared breast with his mouth. About to beg him to do it again, Mead abruptly spun her around and, breaking the kiss, crushed her against his pounding heart.

"I'm sorry, I'm sorry." He struggled to catch his breath. "I didn't mean to go this far...to—"

Devan lifted her head. "It's my fault. You couldn't know."

As they stared at each other, Mead lifted a not-quite-steady hand to stroke her hair. "My God," he rasped. "And it was only one night?"

Thirsting anew for him, Devan closed her eyes and nodded.

"There's going to be another."

"I—no, we can't."

"Why not? You're free. I'm free. And it's blatantly apparent we could torch the night and then some."

"I know, but I can't be the girl you knew."

"And who was she?"

"Hot. Curious, and in lust," she admitted wryly.

His chest rose and fell on a not-quite-steady breath. "Those are damned desirable qualities."

"Mead, I can't afford an affair with anyone. First and foremost, my daughter has one parent left, and she hasn't been seeing enough of me. Second, my in-laws, while supportive, are increasingly...well, concerned about that."

"That's why you were crying. Devan, let me help. I happen to have a lot of free time on my hands."

Devan could just imagine what Pamela would say to that. "You're still recovering."

"My doctor told me to work out every day."

"Probably moderately." Devan shook her head. "Regardless, there are other reasons—"

"None that can't be negotiated."

"You don't know that."

With a last, almost fierce kiss, he pushed himself away from the wall, and her. "Thank you."

Bereft at the loss of his heat and passion, a little dazed at the emotions continuing to churn inside her, Devan was slow to reply. "For what?"

"Giving me a reason to keep breathing."

## Chapter Six

"Mr. Regan...are you with me? Breathing?"

Mead stared at Lavender Smart as she reached over the counter to snap her fingers in front of his face. As carefully as possible so as not to scare her with the depth of his concern, he took hold of the hand—at least a pound heavier from all her rings and bracelets—and moved it out of his line of vision.

"What do you mean, Devan went to Emergency? And after *what*?"

"Taking Blakeley to day care. That's what you do with kids before kindergarten so by the time they get there, they know enough about computers to break into the White House's security system." Lavender frowned as he continued to stare at her. "That was a joke, Mr. Regan. Say, you're not liable to go to sleep again, are you?"

About to tell her that he'd suffered from amnesia, not a sleeping sickness, he lost the chance. She rattled on...

"What I'm saying is, Devan's okay. They got the bit of broken thorn out…though they ruined her ring. Snip. Cut it right off. Didn't have a choice as swollen as the finger was getting. It's only a band, though. Not much lost. Heck, even if it was a *ring* ring, she shouldn't be too upset. Bless him, Jay was a good provider, but sorta clueless in other ways, if you catch my drift. Anyway, she'll be here shortly." Lavender fingered one of her sapphire-blue braids while she flipped through old work orders. "I sure am interested in finding out what roses she was working on. I don't see any being planted yesterday. Must've been something she ran into while doing the display over at the King residence."

It was his fault and yet Mead knew he had to keep silent. Devan would be upset if, in trying to take responsibility, he exposed that he'd been at her house again. As it was, he had her friend and partner's mental gears churning fantasies; he could tell by the twinkle in her hazel eyes as she continued to steal glances when she thought he wouldn't notice.

He wanted to do something, get to Devan, but he'd come here on foot and she'd already left the hospital, and he had no idea where it was located. That not-so-small detail made him realize that while he'd come far, he had a good distance to go to feel "normal," whatever that was.

"I'll go wait outside for her," he told Lavender, "so I won't interrupt your work."

"Oh, don't do that, Mr. Regan. Feel free to sit back here at the desk. Would you like some Breakfast Blend?"

"Call me Mead," he replied slowly, not sure if he'd heard correctly. "Breakfast Blend what?"

"Java. Coffee. You partakee of caffeinee?" Lavender giggled at her own humor. "We do the real thing here. Can't you smell it?"

Mead had to smile. Amid all of the floral and spice scents? She had to be kidding. "Thanks. That sounds good."

"Want some creamer? I've got a yummy French vanilla that's practically orgasmic."

"Ah…" Mead cleared his throat. "Black will be fine, thanks."

While Devan's partner hurried to the coffee machine in the back room, Mead took the opportunity to inspect the packed shop. When he was last here, he had been so focused on Devan, he hadn't noticed. Now he saw that a person could spend an hour in the place and not see everything. It looked, he concluded, the way Lavender Smart was dressed—layered and busy, and more than a little fanciful. While it did have its charm, he knew instinctively that Devan didn't have much to do with this part of the business. He paused at the knee-high pooch with the dangling Welcome sign hanging out of its mouth, and was half tempted to bring it home just to see his mother's expression when she saw it outside the front door…or implacable Philo's for that matter. On the table behind it was a carved wood hound with angel wings. Apparently someone liked angels for there were quite a few in the shop, along with rabbits, geese and teddy bears.

"Here you go, hon. Mead. I sure wish I had a doughnut to go with this, but the boys gobble down anything Devan and I bring in the morning."

"Boys?"

"Jorges' crew. He's a citizen, but he's helped us fill our labor needs with young Mexican boys." Lavender sighed. "Most are illegal, but it's not true about what some say on the news. They aren't taking jobs. These kids…they were working brutal hours at some other places near here that I won't mention. Jobs no one born on this side of the border has lasted a week at." She paused, noticing his blank look. "Oh, dear, have I stuck my foot in my mouth? Do you Regans have an interest in those companies, too?"

"I have no idea. Don't worry about it." Mead also had lost most of what he'd known about national, let alone local, politics. "But from the look of those work orders and the size of your nursery out back, it appears you and your employees work hard, too." He'd almost messed up by saying, "From what Devan told me" and took a quick sip of coffee to recover from the close call. For his part, he didn't care who knew he was wholly engrossed, even bewitched, with her; however, her reaction last night warned him to err on the side of discretion about revealing that to anyone else.

Several silver pendants sunk deeper into Lavender's generous cleavage as she drew a deep breath, and the blue bolero top's knot under her breasts was tested, too. "We're feeling blessed that the business is growing as fast as it is, but it needs to because we keep our prices low, which means our profit margin is smaller. Anyway, Enrique and Pasquale are handling the lawn service part of things, and Jorges, Carlos and Manny—that's Manuel—are with Devan doing the landscaping stuff. Well, Devan oversees all of it because she loves the outdoors and—unlike yours truly—she doesn't whine like I do when she destroys her nails," she amended. She wiggled all ten digits whose purple nails matched her flowing peasant dress. Each finger, including her thumb, was adorned with rings.

"She's just amazing with the boys," Lavender continued merrily. "Jorges calls her *Mamasita*, that's little mother, for the way she watches over them and makes sure they have a place to sleep and all. Plus she's insisting they learn English, so they'll have a better chance at getting their citizenship down the road. *Mamasita* nothing, she's the East Texas Dali Lama, making sure they have time and clothes to go to church, practice good hygiene and eat right, scolding them for littering…"

Shaking his head at her ability to get in so many words on one breath, Mead smiled. "How did you two end up as partners?"

Lavender laughed. "She came by my booth at the trades days market once too often. That's where I started out when I first came to town. She was always telling me that I needed to bottle this or market that. She was right, but I was living out of a van and didn't know what credit was, let alone if I had any." Her smile grew a little self-conscious. "I guess I was a Gypsy of sorts. You wouldn't have approved. Your mother still doesn't like me."

Mead took another sip of his coffee. "I wouldn't lose any sleep over that. What's important is that it's clear Devan thinks the world of you, and your store is…amazing."

Her grin returned to full wattage. "Aren't you sweet. Lucky for Devan, I have a boyfriend."

"No, lucky him," Mead replied, saluting her with the foam cup.

"Ha! Wait till I tell him. Can't pass on any opportunity to make him take notice." The phone rang and she patted his arm. "You explore all you want. I can't imagine what's keeping Devan, but knowing her, she's running one more errand before she comes here."

As she went to answer the phone, Mead turned to look out the window, not at all reassured by Lavender's supposition.

Burning mad and humiliated to have been pulled aside by her banker and handed a hot check—even if it wasn't her fault—Devan glared at building developer Riley Walsh in the small glass-enclosed foyer of MV Bank and Trust. "What's going on, Riley?"

Looking fresh from a shower, his outdated pompadour glistening from excessive hair product as much as sunlight, his burnt orange sports coat and camel-brown slacks lacking even a wrinkle from sitting in the car, Riley Walsh appeared as confident as ever. She could tell immediately that he thought having to deal with her was merely an inconvenience.

Rather than answer her question, Riley focused on her bandaged finger. "What's happened to you, darlin'?"

Told by the intern to keep her hand raised or at least vertical as much as possible, Devan tucked it under her other arm. "Nothing much. We have more serious things to discuss. Do I have to spell it out for you?"

"Oh, that." He snorted dismissively.

"Three thousand isn't pocket change by anyone's standards."

"I was about to call Lavender and warn you," he drawled, speaking slowly, as though English was her second language. "There was a documentation glitch and a client's closing was delayed to this afternoon. I shouldn't have jumped the gun and sent you the check, but I knew you girls needed old Riley's support."

Apparently he needed help, too, but she had just enough sense left to resist blurting that out. Granted, she and Lavender were living close-to-the-wire financially, but they were a relatively new business. He was well into his third development and this one was the priciest so far. If he couldn't cover the cost of landscaping a house to look worth its asking price at this stage, something was seriously wrong.

"That still leaves Dreamscapes with a hot check and some bank fees coming down the transom for us, Riley."

"Aw, it was an honest mistake, and soon resolved, as I

said. Wish everything on my plate was. Why, with the mayoral race and the social obligations involved, the Manor Estates project, and the new property I'm negotiating, I'm doing well to know what driveway to pull into at the end of the day," he said, adding a sly wink.

Already turned off by his manner, Devan struggled not to show her distaste and wondered how on earth Pamela Regan could stand this man. The rumors that there was more than politics between them couldn't possibly be true. "Well, how about assuring my banker, Ben James?"

"Tell him to talk to Wally."

Wally Durst was the executive vice president. "He already has. They sit at the same board table during loan committee meetings every morning. An overdraft list is right next to their coffee mugs. If Mr. Durst was going to reassure Ben that your check had overdraft privileges, wouldn't he have told him then?"

"Now, Devan—be sweet. Old Wal's getting on in years and probably had a senior moment."

"Mr. Walsh, I'd appreciate it if you'd remember that we have a business relationship. You're not talking to one of the kids at the doughnut shop who can't make change without the cash register doing the math." It was a bold response, but she resented the way he reverted to redneck sleazeball when dealing with her and particularly Lavender. As for Riley's assumption that he had the executive vice president in his pocket, she knew Ben would give her his utmost support; he'd purchased a Walsh house last year and had an ongoing list of complaints regarding its construction.

Although soured somewhat by her remark, Riley gestured inside. "Let's go talk to Durst. I'll get him to accommodate your overdraft, considering we're both valued customers."

Well, one of them maybe, Devan thought as she accompanied him inside.

Ten minutes later she again left the bank, this time with the reluctant guarantee of the senior loan officer. MV Bank and Trust would cover any problems she experienced in the next twenty-four hours caused by Walsh Development and Construction, Inc.

Had she made a mistake pressing for this, and for not taking any of Riley's good-old-boy attitude and cost them future Walsh business? Maybe…but how good was he if they had to borrow money to make their payroll?

She barely got to the parking lot when she realized that Pamela had arrived and was parking next to her SUV. The only good news about the inevitable confrontation was that she was driving herself for a change. Pamela could be intimidating enough without that spooky Pryce Philo shadowing her.

The petite woman gracefully eased out of the Cadillac, and Devan would have suffered another needle back at Emergency to be dressed in something other than her work jeans and gray Mount Vance Mustangs sweatshirt. In comparison, Pamela wore her trademark color, red, this time an exquisite Chanel-style suit with matching shoes and bag.

"Well. Devan."

"Good morning, Mrs. Regan," she replied, feeling like a schoolgirl caught chewing gum in class. She barely managed to resist adjusting her black baseball cap and smoothing her ponytail.

Arranging a red-and-black shawl artfully around her shoulders, Pamela blinked at her attire. "You're off to play in the dirt?"

"Someone has to do it," Devan replied with a stiff smile.

As much as she'd like to say something vastly different, they provided the Regan's lawn service as well as served as Pamela's florist. "Hate to run, but I'm behind schedule." She held up her bandaged finger that so far Pamela had ignored. "Had to make a small detour to Emergency."

"I see. I hope it's nothing serious?"

She'd managed to say that without an ounce of concern, and that had Devan feeling more ill than when Ben showed her Riley's hot check. "No, ma'am. Is there anything else you need for Friday? So far the weather looks terrific for the Chamber banquet." Pamela was a charter member and chairman of this year's decoration committee.

"Come to think of it, I might like a corsage."

There was no question of mentioning cost. Pamela would expect it gratis as a gesture for bringing Dreamscapes the business. "Fine. We'll be happy to accommodate you. What color are you planning to wear?"

"Something seasonal."

"Sounds lovely. I'll tell Lavender."

About to continue to her SUV, Pamela touched her arm. "Yes?"

"I understand my son has sought you out."

"Our paths have crossed once or twice. It's good to see his recovery is going so well."

"Yes." After a slight pause Pamela continued, "Why was he in your shop the other day?"

Devan's face was already warm from the slight fever she'd contracted, a combination of the infection and last night's damp chill worsening her sore throat. Pamela's question upped the heat several degrees and she knew her cheeks had to be flushed. "Oh, Mrs. Regan, I could no more tell you that than I would tell someone your business."

"Your discretion is admirable. I want you to understand,

however, that my son remains—vulnerable. You'll appreciate a mother's concern that he not be taken advantage of."

It was a good thing that Pamela was the one to move on because Devan couldn't think, let alone attempt an escape. Stunned, she had to shake her head to clear it. Had she heard correctly? Did that human cobra just insult her own son's mental capacity as well as threaten her?

Shivering, Devan used the remote on her keychain to unlock the SUV and climbed inside. "My God," she whispered. Dropping her head back against the seat, she closed her eyes.

Increasingly worried, Mead was ready to go back into the shop to ask Lavender to call Devan's cell phone when he saw the white SUV coming down the road. He stepped between two parked cars to meet her.

"I was beginning to think you'd gone back to the hospital or had a flat tire," he said once she'd lowered the window. He pulled on the door handle and found it locked. "Open up, Devan."

Instead she asked, "What are you doing here, Mead?"

"Trying to help you. Will you unlock the door, please?" Mead nodded behind her. "You're blocking traffic."

At that instant the driver of the pickup honked lightly. Muttering under her breath, Devan released the lock and Mead climbed into the passenger seat.

"You look like you're about to pass out," he said, frowning as he studied her. "What all did they do to your finger?"

"Lanced it. Cleaned it out. It's no big deal. Would you please fasten your seat belt?" she said without looking at him. "There's a patrol car a block away and the way I'm going, a ticket would just about finish me off."

"I'd reimburse you."

"That's the least of my worries."

Confused and concerned, Mead obliged, but this wasn't at all the way he had planned the morning to go. Granted, he was glad to meet Lavender and hear her enthusiastic praise and affection for her partner, but he'd been looking forward to searching Devan's eyes in daylight for the pleasure and passion that had been there last night. He wanted her warmth. What he felt now was a wall.

"Lavender says to tell you that Jorges and the crew went on ahead."

"Good. Thanks."

Even so, Devan turned right at the light and another at the next street. Mead was confused. "Where are you going? I thought Lavender said Manor Estates was south of town?"

"It is. I'm taking you home. Well, if you don't mind, I'll drop you off at the park. I do not need to show up at your front gate right now."

Alarm bells were now going off in Mead. Narrowing his eyes, he said, "Something else has happened."

With a brief, mirthless laugh, Devan turned back onto Main Street and headed north. "You can say that again. Look, I'm sorry for sounding on edge, but it's been a genuinely rotten morning. That's no excuse, I know, so if it's any consolation, I'm totally disgusted with myself. And I do appreciate your good intentions. I do. But it's…it's just impossible."

"Pull over."

"Why?"

"Just do it."

"No, Mead. There's no point."

"Pull over, Devan, and talk to me, because I'm not getting out of this vehicle until you do." He had no plans to get out regardless, but he wasn't about to upset her more than she already was.

With an exasperated sigh, she drove another few hundred yards and pulled onto an expanded shoulder that served as the storage area for the county road crews to dump their asphalt. But she only braked. "This is futile. It's not going to change anything," she said, staring straight forward.

In reply, Mead turned the ignition key, killing the engine. Then he shoved the gearshift into park. "You're right. It's not."

About to protest, Devan stopped, slumped back in her seat and covered her face with her hands.

Mead leaned over to slip his hand under her ponytail to massage her neck. "Let me help."

"You can't. That would just make it worse."

Her voice sounded raspy and her skin was feverishly hot. "You should be home in bed, not going to any job site. You're burning up."

"I've had a shot and that's a bottle of antibiotics," she replied, gesturing toward the console. "I'll be fine."

Next to the amber container was her damaged ring. "Does your finger hurt?"

"A little. I've had worse."

"I'm sorry for the ring. I'll get it repaired for you."

"Don't be silly. Why should you?"

"Because it's my fault you were hurt."

"I did it to myself, Mead. And I shouldn't be wearing jewelry on the job in the first place."

"You weren't on the job."

As that truth registered, silence fell between them. It seemed it would last forever until Devan slumped forward on the steering wheel, her head resting on her forearms. "I can't do this. I don't have the strength...or the courage."

Mead reached over and took her injured hand. "First things first," he said, and pressed a kiss into her palm.

"Please don't or you're going to have a puddle on your hands and I will hate myself more."

With reluctance, Mead gave her the space she was asking for, but only physically. "You have to tell me, Devan. I'm lost as it is. Without your input I'll be completely blind."

Moaning, she straightened. "You can't trust me that implicitly! Don't you understand this is the real world, too? Fewer guns and bombs, but people aren't much purer. Little is black and white or gets fixed entirely or fairly. You can't be this good and trusting any more now than before."

"You're warning me. I hear you. So now tell me what happened between the trip to the hospital and here."

"I should have known the one characteristic you wouldn't lose was your resolve."

Drawing a deep breath, she finally told him about the events after she left the hospital. Mead hadn't liked Riley Walsh from the moment he'd met him, so he wasn't surprised to hear he was as sloppy a businessman as he was a person. As for her running into his mother...

"Were you nice?" Mead tried for a moment of levity despite suspecting Devan's sense of humor had been annihilated hours ago.

"My mother's people may not have been from *Old Virginia* as hers were, but they were proud Southerners, too, Mead, and believe it or not, the older I get, the more I find myself enjoying the tradition of courtesy and manners. Until someone takes that for granted and crosses the line."

"Did she?"

"Let's just say she asked about you."

Mead could only imagine what that entailed. "Sorry about that. It didn't help that we were both coming in from opposite ends of the house last night, and I was still ...well, thinking about you."

Her condition didn't allow her to grow pale, but Devan's expression shared enough of her sense of doom. "No doubt she asked you where you'd been. What did you tell her?"

"What I had been telling her—that I'm continuing to acclimate." Mead went back to massaging her neck; he couldn't resist touching her, not considering their close proximity. "Didn't I say this clear enough last night? It'll be all right."

Devan's expression remained blank, but her breathing calmed. "We'll see. I guess, aside from everything else, I'm a little embarrassed, too."

"Because we kissed?"

"Mead, that went beyond kissing. In another minute we could have ended up with identical social security numbers."

"So?" He shifted in his seat to better face her. "I've been in contact with plenty of women during my recovery—nurses, doctors, therapists, military personnel...there were opportunities. Nothing tempted me to go there. I noticed how attractive they were—nothing is wrong with my eyes—but no one has made me fantasize the way you did.

"I know that makes you uneasy and that my timing is bad," Mead continued, "but from my position, it's the only time. What if I'd come back and you were still happily married?"

"Then this conversation would never happen."

"Maybe, but you couldn't have stopped me from looking...and wanting. At the risk of complicating your life further, and possibly scaring you, I have no intention of staying away from you, Devan."

"You sound as though you're trying to talk yourself into believing you were in love with me, Mead."

"What if that's true?"

"Because I'm the one who remembers the truth." Finally, she faced him. "At the risk of hurting your feelings, the only reason I went with you to that hotel the night before you last left here was because I knew it would be our only time. I already knew you were a gentleman in that you were discreet, but being aware that you didn't plan to return cinched things."

"I'd said something to indicate the mission would be dangerous?"

"Vets knew by your patches and ribbons that all of your missions were dangerous. But I'd also overheard you'd had a whopper of an argument with your mother. Add that 'commitment' wasn't in your vocabulary and it was a sure bet that what happened between us would stay between us."

"Okay, but what if I fell for you then? What if once we kissed, once we were in bed, and I was inside you, everything changed?"

Devan held his gaze for the first time since last night. "Then it would cast a shadow on the last six years of my life. It would also trigger the What-if? question I've kept so successfully buried."

## *Chapter Seven*

Mead sighed. "I'm sorry again. I didn't mean to embarrass you, but I had to know."

The SUV's interior was at a pleasant 74 degrees, and yet Devan's sweatshirt was beginning to stick to her like flypaper. "I understand. You deserve to know the truth. But I doubt many people are going to be willing to give it to you. There are more skeletons in Southern closets than any New York bank has accounts."

"I'm only interested in one person's truth."

Devan stared at the ruined ring on the console. "You weren't in love with me, Mead."

"But doesn't it strike you interesting that any question I have, virtually every thought, involves you?"

"I don't know what else I can tell you."

"How did we end up together that night?"

She winced. "Jay and I quarreled. He didn't like to go

out to clubs, didn't like to dance, but it was my birthday and I did. I guess the other Devan was rebelling. What with not having a father figure, I thought I enjoyed letting Jay make an increased number of decisions in our relationship. He was doing so well with his businesses, why not? I told myself he was taking care of me. And in his own way, he was. But that night he pushed a little too hard, and the more he did, the more I resisted." She shrugged. "I didn't even finish my second wine spritzer when he told me that I was acting silly and that we were leaving. I was high, all right— on enjoying myself, on letting my hair down, so to speak. And when he left, I didn't follow."

"He left you? Without a ride home?"

"There were people there that we both knew. One of the waitresses was a friend, and so was the bartender. I could have gotten a ride. You were there, too."

As though he couldn't keep from touching her, Mead stroked her ponytail, then twirled a tendril around his index finger. "I'll just bet I was. How long were you alone before I made my move?"

"Maybe five minutes. You waited until I danced with someone. You noticed I'd stopped being happy and came over to ask if something was wrong." Devan smiled. "You were such a gentleman and visibly annoyed that Jay could abandon me. I guess I still seemed a kid to you. That lasted until we danced."

"A slow dance?"

"Very."

Mead stopped playing with her hair only to stroke the curve of her ear, play with the delicate gold ring in her ear. "And every dance after that?"

"No. That was the only one. We both realized there was chemistry. A lot. I told you, you were a gentleman. You weren't going to poach on another man's territory." Devan wished she had that wine he'd bought her before urging her to go visit with some friends who had come in. His touch was turning her throat desert dry even without it being sore.

Mead frowned. "Did I leave?"

"No, you stayed at the bar and drank. You were heading overseas in the morning and I guess you didn't want to spend it back at the house."

"Drank and watched you dance, I'll bet?"

"Uh-huh." She had to open the bottle of water on the console. "There's more, if you want one, in the cooler behind your seat."

"I'm fine, thanks." He waited until she was replacing the top. "It sounds like some serious flirting was going on."

"Oh, yeah." She sighed. "Then, suddenly, you left. I felt—I didn't let myself think. I just followed."

"You felt what?"

"It was as though I could read your mind as clearly as my own."

"I wanted you and got the hell out of there before I did something about it."

She peered at him from under her lashes. "And I wanted you to ask. At that point I didn't intend to go through with it, but I just wanted Mead Regan to make a serious pass at silly little me."

Mead coughed into his fist and shifted uncomfortably. "Honey, I think I'd already made that pass. At least two of them. A guy doesn't approach a woman who's spoken for, and he sure doesn't ask her to dance—especially a slow dance. Not unless desire is overriding his judgment."

"Yeah, but while I wasn't a virgin, my experience was so narrow. What did I know?" She laughed at her own naiveté to keep from dwelling on the intoxicating excitement of feeling him grow aroused as they'd danced, and then hold her closer still to watch her response in her eyes. Never before or since had she felt as alive and aware of her sexuality as when in Mead's arms.

Slipping his index finger under her chin, he coaxed her to look at him again. "When did it finally register that I was serious?"

"Out at your car when you kissed me," she whispered.

Mead gently stroked her lower lip with his thumb. "I'd walk through fire to remember that."

"It blew my mind. I followed you outside and asked you for a ride home. At least, I told myself that's what I was doing. Then we kissed and you said, 'Tempting Devan, if you get in my car, you are *not* going home.' I did, and we didn't." She eased away from his touch as a cloud shadowed her memories. "Guess you know what kind of a girl that made me."

Mead grunted his dismissal. "Were you engaged?"

"No, but it seemed that's where things were heading."

"He abandoned you. As I see it, you'd as good as split up."

Devan cast him a grateful smile. "I told you that you were a gentleman."

"I'm not feeling like one right now." He shifted his hand back behind her neck to pull her toward him.

"Mead, I've got a sore throat and I'm probably coming down with a cold."

"Sweetheart, I've been all but blown to hell, I'm not afraid of a little cold. Come here, Tempting Devan. I need that gorgeous mouth under mine."

She let him, because despite her protests last night, she wanted this, wanted him more.

They didn't need teasing kisses this time; their conversation had brought them both to an emotional wave already halfway to cresting. As he pressed his mouth to hers, she eagerly welcomed him. The kiss went on and on, one moment almost greedy, the next heartbreakingly sweet in its tenderness. If it wasn't for their seat belts, Devan knew that it wouldn't be just their mouths raising the temperature in the SUV.

When Mead tore his lips from hers to breathe, the sensual assault didn't end, he simply drove her to distraction by nuzzling her ear. "I laid awake last night trying to remember," he said with an ache-filled sigh. "I thought, prayed, that with what you'd told me it would all come back."

"You were wonderful." She stroked his cheek. "Unforgettable."

"Did we talk like this?"

"Yes. You liked it. You encouraged me to do more."

"So I told you what I wanted?"

"And urged me to show you what I wanted."

"Show me again," he murmured, returning to her lips.

The kiss didn't help take the edge off the hunger growing between them—it intensified it. Behind her closed lids, Devan relived his other kisses when his mouth, alternately merciless and merciful, set her entire body on fire. Moaning, she trembled and this time she broke the kiss to hide her face against his shoulder.

"Tell me," he coaxed. "You were just remembering, weren't you?"

"We have to stop."

"As attuned as we are just kissing," Mead said, stroking her hair, "the rest must have shot us straight to heaven."

"Yeah."

"What did I say afterward?" he asked.

"No, more," Devan replied, realizing her mistake. "I've got to—"

Gently but firmly, Mead trapped her head between his hands. "Tell me. The words belong to me, too."

"Yes, but I knew not to take what you said too much to heart."

His gruff whispers weren't just branded in her mind, they were in her soul. She heard their echoes in her dreams. He'd been hovering over her, resting his weight on his forearms to look into her eyes as though he couldn't imprint them well enough into his mind. They were both panting and the sheets had started to stick to their passion-soaked bodies. And yet he'd remained hard and throbbing inside her.

Suddenly he'd cursed and rasped, "What lousy timing. What unbelievably bad timing." And then he'd begun surging into her again until they couldn't have spoken if they'd dared risk saying anything more.

When Devan shared that, albeit reluctantly, Mead slowly nodded. A sad smile curved his lips and warmed his eyes as he brushed his thumbs over her cheeks.

Devan had never let herself wonder what he'd meant, what he'd been thinking…at least not until months after Jay's death…after she'd heard Mead lay in a hospital bed probably dying, too. But he was very much alive, and reality demanded that once and for all she take off those rose-colored glasses that tempted her so.

"It's a romantic thought, Mead, but you were a strong man in virtually every way, not just in passion. You would never let down your guard that far."

"You think we always get to choose who we fall in love with and when?"

"We were caught up in a moment. You were already on an adrenaline rush, knowing where you were heading."

"You're so generous in every other way, why are you so rigid about this?"

"Because I'm the person who remembers."

When her gaze finally fell to the clock on the dashboard, she groaned, knowing Jorges was probably on the phone with Lavender this minute. She would never hear the end of her teasing. Reaching for the ignition key, she heard Mead swear.

"Please don't say anything more. I've already stolen more time than I should have," she told him.

"Look to your left," he told her.

She did and gasped. To her dismay Rhys was easing his patrol car beside them. As he lowered his window, he eyed both of them with a mixture of speculation and growing amusement.

Devan quickly keyed the engine and brought her window down, as well. "Hi, Rhys."

"Everything all right?"

Hardly. Wondering how much he'd seen, she moistened her kiss-swollen lips and wished she could make herself vanish. "Sure. Uh, this is Mead Regan. Mead, Rhys Atwood."

Mead nodded. "Lavender's motorcycle man."

She choked.

"What's that?" Rhys asked over his radio that had suddenly come on with a message.

Rhys wasn't quite as dark-haired as Mead, but Devan knew he was a few inches taller—a perfect match to almost six-foot-tall Lavender. Until Mead filled out a few pounds, Rhys could probably best him in strength, too, even if Mead remembered any of his defensive training.

"Please behave," she whispered to Mead. To Rhys, she explained, "Mead just met Lavender this morning. I told him you two were seeing each other."

Nodding, Rhys continued to observe Mead. "So you're not having engine trouble? Not going to Manor Estates today?"

"Right after I drop off Mead."

As she pointed, Rhys saw the bandage. "What happened to your finger?"

Devan could tell he was trying to decide if she was performing under duress or not. She tried to settle her jangling nerves. She liked Rhys a lot and knew he was just doing his job; she didn't want the last week's experiences to reflect negatively on Mead.

"Hazards of the job—infection. You boys in blue aren't the only ones in danger," she teased. "I was looking at a staph infection thanks to a killer thorn."

He grimaced. "Lousy luck. I know how backed up you are work-wise. Well, you take care of it—and you."

As he pulled away and continued with his patrol, Devan reached for the stick shift. The way she slammed it into drive had Mead covering her hand with his.

"Why are you upset?"

"Because he'll tell Lavender. And she'll tease." And speculate.

"Let her. It's not like I'm going to disappear. And you're not taking me home." Mead nodded at her wound. "It sounds like everyone knows you're in need of help and now that you're down to one hand and I've used up more of your time, pushing me away is a luxury you can't afford."

"But your mother—"

"One thing at a time. Look at it this way," he said, leaning back in his seat and folding his arms over his chest, "if you insist on doing this? I'll get there on my own. Your call."

Almost fifteen minutes later Devan turned into Lafayette Lane. "We're here."

It was the first thing she'd said since she'd cut a U-turn and driven south.

Mead knew he was responsible for a great deal of her tension, but he was convinced he was right to coerce her to accept his help. Okay, bully her into it, he thought ruefully, and right now she needed lots of TLC, not that. But at least he was here to keep an eye on her and make sure she didn't injure herself further, or drop from exhaustion. The rest he'd fix somehow—and work on soothing her concerns about his presence in her life.

The "here" she referred to turned out to be a sprawling Spanish white-brick hacienda with an adobe-tiled roof and a circular drive leading to a courtyard entrance. Mead had seen some advertisements for Walsh houses in his mother's study. What Pamela was doing with them he didn't know, unless it was to have the literature handy when she was campaigning on his behalf. Mead had to admit this several-acre estate was the most impressive. A Dreamscapes van was parked in the driveway and plants, sacks of mulch and tools were spread everywhere.

"I hate to give Walsh points," he said conversationally, "but this is quite a place."

After a slight hesitation, Devan replied, "The inside is even better. If one of the other contractors is around, you should take a look. It's a lovely mix of Santa Fe desert and East Texas piney woods."

Although she sounded almost formally polite, he was grateful she was at least talking, and made another observation. "You sound like you wished it was yours."

"Hardly."

"Because of any profit Walsh would get out of that?"

"It's just ridiculously large for two people. Besides, it would eat my daughter's college fund as well as the proceeds from the sale of our house. Add that there was a contract pending when I first came to plan the landscape, and I didn't let myself begin to get tempted."

In more ways than one, Mead thought, filing away the information. One thing he was learning about Devan was how she tried to keep herself strictly disciplined. She could give Philo a good challenge. "How many of these has he built?"

"He told me today that he's negotiating his third project," she replied, killing the engine. "I'd say that's about twenty houses."

That really caught his attention and Mead understood why she'd looked ready to shatter when he'd first seen her. "You had to deal with Riley and my mother in one morning on top of that?" he said, nodding to her bandaged finger.

"And a hot check from him." As Mead's concerned expression turned into a full-fledged scowl, she sighed. "I considered telling you, but you'd just react the way you are."

"There's something wrong with me being concerned and upset for you?"

Glancing past him out the passenger window, she hedged. "I have to get out there. My people are starting to wonder what's going on."

As Devan climbed out of the SUV, Mead followed suit and met her at the rear. "Will you be all right? What the hell is wrong with the guy? You'd think he would be pretty damned solvent by now."

"You can't say anything I haven't thought since the first insufficient funds problem."

"First?" Mead had to grit his teeth not to utter more than a curse. "I've had an unpleasant feeling whenever I've been around him."

"It's none of my business, and I don't mean to offend,

so feel free to say so, but do you think he and your mother are having an affair? He's married, you know. Three kids, all in college. That may explain his problematic cash flow. Trying to impress a mistress on top of all that…"

"Until now I'd have laughed at the idea. All I can say is, if she's so desperate to get involved with that piece of slime, she deserves whatever happens."

As he opened the tailgate for her, Devan touched Mead's arm. "Please don't say anything to your mother. Not about the check or the other."

Something twisted inside his chest. "You called me a gentleman. How can you begin to think I would even consider breaking your trust?"

She quickly leaned into the SUV and, for anyone looking, Mead knew it looked as though she was simply reaching for something amid all the boxes and equipment she had packed back there. But he had caught a glimpse of her blinking back tears before she'd spun away.

He used his body to give her as much privacy as possible. "God, Devan. I didn't mean it the way that sounded."

"I'm sorry." Her voice vibrated with tears. "I'm so not ready for these emotions."

"I've been greedy of your time." Wanting any and all information she could provide him, wanting her. "If you'll tell me what you want to unload and hand me over to your foreman, I'll stay out of your way."

She drew a deep breath. "That's unfair and unnecessary—you're here for me. I just have to be tougher, to make a few calls.

"As Lavender probably told you, our foreman is Jorges. Lovely family man who brings us reliable workers." She nodded to where three men worked. "He's the one with the black cowboy hat directing the two elbow deep in mulch. They're Manuel and Carlos, probably illegal despite their ID. Usually, our people come from the chicken farms and plants. They've had their fill of the work for any number of reasons. We can't pay what they've been earning there, but the environment is a thousand percent better and not likely to do them in health-wise. C'mon," Devan said, "I'll introduce you."

Mead followed as promised, but he also noticed she did her best to avoid physical contact. "How did you get involved with this business?"

"It was either this or become a county-western star. That's a joke," she added quickly. "Good grief, I couldn't make junior high choir. It was during a science project when I stuck toothpicks in an avocado pit and mine was the only one to sprout that I figured I'd been shown my calling. As soon as my mother noticed kids bringing me seeds to grow for them, she bought me a terrarium. It's in Blakeley's room now. She winters chameleons."

"More kidding?"

"Her grandparents wish. I'm hoping I have a biologist on my hands, but I'm realistic. Unlike me, she *can* sing, and they're coaxing her to try piano lessons, so I may end up with another Norah Jones."

They continued to the front of the house and Mead processed the emotions rushing through him. Most were positive—he wanted to hear more about her childhood and her little girl. But they were stepping under the adobe arbor and into the courtyard where three other pairs of eyes were suddenly on him—all more suspicious than curious.

"Jorges, Carlos, Manuel…this is *señor* Mead Regan.

He's going to help with the work. *Mi mano esta mala.*"
Holding up her hand, she'd explained in their native
Spanish that she had injured herself. "Will you show him
what's to be done, Jorges?"

"*Sí, señora.* One problem though…we got no water."

## *Chapter Eight*

Middle-aged and heavily mustached Jorges wasn't much taller than Devan, yet for all of his gruffness, Mead noticed that whenever the foreman spoke to her, he touched two fingers to his black-felt cowboy hat in deference, and when he watched her, it was with genuine affection. After hearing how her day had been going and witnessing the toll it was taking on her—a good portion his own fault—he approved of the foreman within minutes of shaking his hand.

However, he feared for Devan, Jorges' news about the water could have been the severing of her last nerve.

"We were promised it would be on," she said, gingerly plucking out a phone from her jeans. "The plumbing is supposed to be tested today." Flipping open the phone and murmuring, "Excuse me," she exited the courtyard.

As she left, Mead said to her foreman, "Is there a second source of water nearby?"

Jorges pointed to the more modern three-story next door. "Them. But they don't like us going there."

"Same builder?"

"No, *señor.*"

"Call me Mead." Hoping he wouldn't be causing more trouble than help, Mead was willing to try to get them temporarily out of their bind. "If you're willing, I could go and explain the situation. What do you see as the best way to get you what you need? More hoses, or would a few of those buckets there work?"

"We plant mostly cactus in here," Jorges replied, polite, but still reserved. "Buckets be good."

"Okay. Let's see what I can do."

"*¡Gracias!*" Jorges said, giving him the thumbs up signal.

Several minutes later Mead returned and waved to signal his success to the foreman, then went over to Devan, who was just ending a call. "You're good to go next door for the water. Jorges can have his people drive the van up to the front faucet and take all they need."

Her exasperation was barely contained. "It's the name thing again, isn't it? That crew has been so grouchy, you'd think they were competing with us on some TV reality show."

"I have no idea if he knew the name, but he recognized the twenty dollar bill I slipped him."

Devan lifted her eyebrows. "You bribed him?"

"Didn't see as I had a choice. He turned down dinner with my mother."

Devan's mouth opened as though she was going to protest, then she burst into laughter. "I hope you're kidding?" When he only shrugged, she sighed. "What am I going to do with you?"

His imagination went immediately into overdrive.

"Boss, if you want me to be able to focus on my job," he drawled, "try not to ask me such loaded questions."

For the next hour Mead and the two younger boys hauled the water they needed, and finished the planting, while Jorges worked on the outside of the courtyard filling the mailbox planter with the proper combination of soil and mulch, then plants. When they were through, they started laying a solid blanket of grass from the two pallets of sod lined up on the sidewalk. Once Devan finished catching up with her phone messages, she and Jorges drove to their next location to double check what they would be planting there. They then switched vehicles and returned to Dreamscapes to load everything.

Mead enjoyed the physical activity and could feel it did his recuperating body good to be outdoors in the fresh air and sunshine and not just exercising on some indoor machine. That his efforts steadily gained him increased acceptance from Devan's crew was a bonus.

It was noon when he noticed her drive off yet again in the SUV, only to return in a half hour with a restocked cooler of water, soft drinks and a bag of submarine sandwiches and chips. She said something in Spanish to her crew, then gave him a little tilt of her head that told him that he needed to follow her.

"You treat your people well," he said when they were out of hearing range. From her troubled expression, he knew something else had happened.

"We've been working with the boys for almost a year, and Jorges from the beginning. He's practically family, and they're good kids and homesick," she replied matter-of-factly. "It's the least we can do to show our appreciation." At the SUV she paused and crossed her arms to create a brace for her injured hand.

"Don't you think you should give up the good fight and take something for the pain?" Mead asked. She hadn't given any other sign that she was hurting, but he saw the bit of red coming through her bandage and suspected she overdid it loading plants. Jorges wasn't a youngster and no way would she let him do it by himself no matter how much the foreman may have protested.

"I will soon." She nodded at her vehicle. "There's a sandwich in there for you. We need to go."

"Why do I get the feeling that you don't mean the hospital or some scenic little spot where I can kiss you better?"

"Mead…" She rubbed her forehead with the back of her hand. "God, this has been an insane morning. I'm so grateful for your help this morning, but I need to get you back to your place and pronto. Your mother's butler or chauffeur, or whatever you call him—"

"What about Philo?" The mere thought of her having any contact with the enigmatic man had him tensing.

"Why does that name make me feel like I'm saying Fido when he looks more like a bulldog?"

"Because you have good instincts. I suspect that before coming here he was either in my former line of work or the pen."

Devan searched his face as though trying to decide whether he was serious or kidding. "Mead, he's looking for you. Don't you have a phone?"

"No." Nor a renewed license, but he intended to look into both matters soon.

"Well, I was coming out of the sandwich place and he blocked me and questioned me about your whereabouts like some government agent. I'm not sure he believed me when I told him that I had no idea. I have to admit that I was unnerved by him."

He dared treat her that way? Mead seethed inwardly. "Did he touch you?"

"No. But he didn't have to, to get my attention."

Hoping she didn't see the cold intent settling inside him, he briefly squeezed her upper arm. "I'm sorry. I promise you that it won't happen again. Let's go."

Once inside the SUV, Devan cast him a worried look. "You're not going to do anything excessive, are you?"

"He intimidated you. That's unacceptable. And I'm not a lost lapdog or some kid. It's none of his business where I go."

"Maybe not, but it is your mother's. She has a right to be concerned considering your health."

"My health is *fine*. Hell, I've even gained two pounds in the last few days." Maybe he still regretted having given Blakeley a scare and upsetting Devan, but meeting her again had been the best thing to happen to him. He wouldn't lose her a second time.

Mead had Devan drop him off at the entrance to the mansion's road instead of the park. He figured since it was the lunch hour, and the weather mild, the park would be busier with those who were eager to take advantage and enjoy a last picnic, or to burn off their lunch calories. That still gave him close to a mile to walk. He was halfway to his destination when the familiar Cadillac pulled up from behind him.

"I'm impressed," Philo began as Mead settled beside him in the passenger seat. "Such a small town and modest population, yet you managed to stay one step ahead of me."

"Where is she?" Mead asked, ignoring the question behind the observation.

"At the house. She canceled a luncheon appointment for you."

More than likely she'd gotten wind of the news about Walsh's latest financial problem and she was avoiding embarrassing questions by other abused creditors. He knew better than to ask Philo to confirm that, though. Besides, they had another issue to discuss.

"Where did you work before you came here?" he asked.

"It's on the confidential résumé I gave to Mrs. Regan."

Undoubtedly interesting reading: how much of it was fabricated would also be fascinating. "Sounds like a sweet arrangement—she keeps your secrets and you do her bidding."

Pulling up to the electronic gate, Philo cast him a mild look before clicking the remote. "I don't blame you for being out of sorts, but let me reassure you that I was only doing my job—as economically as possible—to return to where I could do the most good. By the way, was that Mrs. Anderson in that white Navigator I saw a few miles back? It's a shame considering the embarrassment she caused you and your mother that she didn't offer you a lift home."

Mead was beginning to understand how this game was played, and he wasn't going to make Devan any more vulnerable than she already was. But as his mother's right hand drove through the open gate, he issued the strongest warning he could. "The next time you're ordered to stick your nose in my business do yourself a favor, buy yourself an ice cream and take a drive farther out into the country until you change your mind."

"I don't like ice cream."

"And I don't like you. But occasionally we all have to deal with the unpleasant…or suffer the consequences, don't we?"

"Food for thought."

"Damned straight."

As soon as Philo stopped the car, Mead climbed out and

went to deal with his mother. He found her in the study on the phone and more than a little agitated.

"What do you mean, there's been an unavoidable change of plans? This is one of the year's biggest events and may I remind you that thanks to me you're up for an award? Winning isn't the point. It's important that you're seen as involved." Spotting Mead in the doorway, she quickly changed her tone. "I have to go. Hugs to you, too. See you tomorrow. *Call me the moment you return.*"

Watching as she slammed down the phone, he raised an eyebrow. "Lover's spat?"

"What?" Momentarily startled, Pamela quickly recovered. "Don't be ridiculous. Or evasive. I'm extremely displeased with you. Your conduct forced me to cancel a meeting and a luncheon. Mead, this cannot continue."

Although she slapped the desk with the flat of her hand, he made sure he remained blank-faced and seemingly unperturbed. "And what would 'this' be precisely?"

"Your complete disregard and disrespect for my responsibilities and indifference to my concern over you." She frowned, taking in his appearance. "Good grief—where have you been? Don't you dare sit on a single piece of furniture in this house without first showering."

"Why don't I just hose myself down outside?"

Pamela reacted as though she'd found a fly in her tea. "Watch your smart mouth, mister."

"Why don't we get to the point and stop wasting each other's time," he said, crossing his arms over his chest. "What right do you have to police my every move?"

His mother pressed a hand over her heart. "'Police?' I'm worried sick you've had one of your white-out moments in the middle of Main Street and you accuse me of that?"

"I don't have white-out moments."

"Until recently that's all you've had. Even the doctors at the last hospital said you would stay in a trancelike state for hours."

"Hasn't it occurred to you that I might have an aversion to meaningless chatter?"

His mother didn't go into another rant, as he expected, or try another tack and burst into tears. She simply stood and studied him quietly.

"I want my son back," she said at last.

"For better or worse," Mead drawled, arms akimbo, "you got your wish."

She shook her head. "We used to be friends. We enjoyed each other's company."

Mead couldn't buy that. Why then would he spend his last night home in a bar, as Devan had said?

"Your father used to be so proud of us, even a little envious."

What the hell was going on? he wondered. She hadn't mentioned his father once since he'd come home except to explain the II at the back of his birth certificate when he'd asked.

"If I've seemed a little overly protective lately," she continued, "it's only because I'm the one who knows what's been taken from me, and it's very painful."

And yet Mead didn't sense one iota of real feeling coming from her. He wished he did. Had he become the type of soldier he'd been because he'd inherited the worst of her genes and didn't give a damn about anything, or anyone, except achieving a goal? If that was true, he could almost be grateful for what had happened to him.

"That's no excuse to send Philo after me the way you did."

"But, dear, how else was I to be reassured that you were all right?"

"I'll get a phone."

"Excellent. I was thinking of that myself. Philo knows everything about electronics."

I'll just bet he does, Mead thought.

"He can—"

"I'll take care of it myself," he told her.

Pamela blinked, but her pleased smile came quickly. "Thank you. So who did you see today? Did you come across any old friends?"

She was, Mead thought, as graceful as a shark slicing through the water. "Rhys Atwood," he replied, sensing it was smart to throw her some kind of bone.

"Oh, he couldn't be a friend, darling, he's only been in Mount Vance a few months. Why did he speak to you?"

"I guess he'd heard about me and asked if I was okay."

"How thoughtful."

"Who was on the phone?" Mead asked, matching her pleasant tone.

"Oh…my cochair for the chamber banquet tomorrow night. It's so frustrating, but she's dumping all the work in my lap and going out of town. What's more, I'll have an empty seat right beside me." Crooning, Pamela clasped her hands. "Darling, under the circumstances, would you consider taking her place? I'd be so grateful, as well as honored. And it would be the perfect opportunity for the who's who to see how you've rebounded."

"Haven't we had this discussion before?"

"All right," she sighed. "I'm disappointed, but I respect your decision. I'm sure at least one person will be sorry that you're not there."

"Who?"

Pamela smiled.

* * *

"Sure, go ahead and make me feel like a slug," Lavender said, putting yet another arrangement into one of the display coolers. "Devan, I've been able to sit down when I'm tired and still work. You started out in Emergency *and* put in a full, physical hauling-and-digging day. I can't let you stay and help with these late orders. But I'm gonna squeeze you to pieces for offering."

Devan chuckled and protested through her partner's effusive display of affection. "Crazy woman," she replied once she was freed. "You know Blakeley is at her grandparents' because it's Jerrold's birthday and Connie insisted. Mead was a great help this morning, and I caught up on a lot of other work. Let's split the orders you have left and you may get home in time to make Rhys smile."

"Ha! He'll smile no matter what time I get there. But speaking of…you should have heard what he said about seeing you today," Lavender purred. She headed for the refrigerator. "Let me get you a glass of wine and me a margarita first."

Devan couldn't help smiling. "Just half a glass. I'm on meds. And be nice. It's not like I didn't tell you about Mead."

"He was nice. So will I be. He said Mead was decent and that you looked really buzzed."

"'Buzzed'?"

"I'll interrogate him later for details. He sounded like he was grinning like a fool when he called. He also said he likes you with more color in your face. He thinks you've been so pale this year. I agree."

Devan figured there was a benefit to being tired; she didn't have the energy to worry over what would be forthcoming from those two in the future. "Well, now that the peanut gallery has been heard from, why don't I take these two golden anniversary orders and the birthday one? That should free you up to handle the rest of the Polk funeral orders you've been working on."

"If your hand isn't giving you too much trouble, I'd appreciate it."

It was stiff and swollen, but she'd experienced much worse. "Consider it done. You know another reason I wanted to stay is that we need to talk business, too."

"I'd rather know what Mead said. Shoot, I *really* want to know what he did."

Devan accepted the glass her friend passed her and redirected her back to priorities. "I mean, about getting you help. We're stretched so thin we're going to have to say we can't take business soon, and that's when we start losing money. We've plateaued, which is good, but could get problematic in a heartbeat. You need help here in the shop."

"Not just here. Old Butch, who's been watching the nursery on our busiest days, hasn't been showing up. He didn't want any steady or serious work to protect his social security, but I didn't realize that meant getting virtually no work out of him whatsoever. I didn't want to heap worry onto you, but he hasn't bothered to show up the last two days."

"Then I guess you should put a Help Wanted sign in the window out back."

"People wander in and halfheartedly ask, but I just don't respond to their vibes, Devan. You know I'm easy as sin to work with."

"If you like twenty-four-hour TV and radio simultaneously."

"It's good to keep informed. I can make small talk with—"

"Yourself." Devan had lost count of how many times she'd come upon Lavender having in-depth conversations and no one else had been in the building. But as she chose the vase for the first arrangement, she remembered something. "Nina," she said, turning back to her partner. "Jorges was just saying that she was trying to earn money to back up the college scholarships she's applied for, but you know what's available in town—flip burgers, slice pizza or scoop ice cream. You know she's learned at the elbow of the best cook around, her mama. She'd like to make the maximum use of her time and take on something new."

The teenager was lovely, the only girl and youngest child; nevertheless, she'd grown up against type and there was nothing spoiled or coddled about her.

Her dream was to own a business someday. Exactly what she hadn't yet decided.

Lavender sipped at her margarita, then retrieved a wire frame for an ivy and rose funeral tribute. "You know I think she's adorable. Jorges and his whole family did a super job raising all their kids, but if we're going to do this, shouldn't we look for someone who can work more than an hour or two a day? And is she going to be willing to give up her weekends for a job? A looker like her?"

"She's an achiever," Devan replied. "And she has so many credits built up she gets first and second period virtually to work at what she wants."

"That's better. Plus we already know each other's personalities. Yeah, I'd be willing to give it a try."

"Terrific." Devan went to choose flowers for her arrangement among the chrysanthemums and red baby roses. Another problem solved. If only she could be sure that Mead was getting along half as well.

## Chapter Nine

They'd run out of burgundy and gold ribbon thanks to their order being shortchanged by their suppliers, and—because it was football season and there were several schools with one or the other of those colors—it was no surprise that they couldn't get more. That left Devan and Lavender scrambling. They all but cleaned out their shop and the local fabric store to get enough material closely matching each color to finish off the head table and those framing it. The rest of the tables were draped in white linen with burgundy napkins and gold accents.

Stretching her back to ease the ache brought on by the pace they'd kept particularly in the last forty-eight hours, Devan scanned the banquet hall where the Chamber of Commerce would shortly be holding its annual dinner. It looked quite nice, she thought. Less autumnal than planned, but more elegant with the extra baskets of burgundy chrysanthemums and the bouquets of burgundy and white mums on every table; and who could deny the touches of crystal from Devan's own china hutch didn't add glimmer to the tired old building? Would Event Chair Pamela Regan approve, though?

"Well, you know I'm not a traditionalist, but if Rhys proposed tonight, I'd rent this for my a.m. engagement party," Lavender said with starry eyes.

"If we survive this, don't look for me there," Devan replied, stifling a yawn. "I plan to be out of commission and dead to the world until nine and if Blakeley rings me sooner, she's going up for adoption." She'd made a deal with Lavender to stay and clean up tonight so that Lavender could go home but would run the store on Saturday, the half day they were open.

"We'll miss you, but you deserve the rest. I simply did not see this. Goes to show you that I'm just the see-the-trees person and you're the forest-and-then-some. Wow, Devan, a person could almost forget we're in this old wreck of a barn."

The city had been talking for years to update or replace the auditorium, but funds had not been forthcoming for numerous reasons. Devan didn't understand how the community could hold up its head in the county, let alone the state, and not support a center that represented themselves with pride.

"This is *not* what we ordered."

At the sound of Pamela Regan's voice, Devan spun around. Pamela, and behind her Mead, stood resplendent like royalty at a ball. Pamela was in a formal-length crème and cranberry gown and Mead in a black suit. As good as he looked, Devan wondered if his mother wasn't disappointed that he wasn't wearing his dress uniform. What she was trying to understand was why he'd agreed to come at all.

"Mrs. Regan," she said to fill the uneasy silence, "you look lovely."

"I look like the tablecloths!"

So she did, and Devan couldn't do anything but look on in horror. They'd discussed her outfit and Lavender had put together a darling corsage in shades of rust, amber, yellow and crème. As Lavender held the box out to the woman, she wasn't surprised to see her recoil.

"We discussed what you'd be wearing," Devan reminded her.

"You shouldn't have relied on your memory and taken notes." Pulling herself together for another regal review, Pamela all but sniffed her disdain. "I don't know how you could have misunderstood our requirements, as well. This will be reviewed before your invoice is processed, but I suppose we'll have to suffer through the night as best as we can."

"It's freaking good!" Lavender huffed under her breath.

"The tables look especially nice," Mead said. "What on earth is this place?"

While Lavender snickered, Devan considered kissing him on the spot.

"You don't understand, son," Pamela stated, striding forward among the tables to give an official review. "It's an historic site. The first settlers of Mount Vance spent their initial winter here."

"It smells like not all of them left," Lavender muttered to Devan.

Pamela swung around and pointed up front. "The head table was to have a full accent over the skirt. You're at least eight feet short and that material looks…well it's a mess. You might as well have stapled a pile of tutus to the thing. I'll remind you, we have a contract. As far as I'm concerned you failed to meet our specifications."

"A contract with a clause for contingencies, ma'am. Those came into play."

Pamela stared hard. "Be assured the chamber board will look into them and ask for a full explanation and supporting documentation." She glanced over at Lavender. "Are you willing to put your future into her hands?"

"Oh, Ms. Regan," Lavender replied in a twangy drawl, "my future has been in the hands of brain-fried flower children, cultists, scam artists and your run-of-the-mill bums. I'm fearless."

It was the worst thing she could say as far as Devan was concerned.

Pamela pulled herself to her maximum height, although even benefited by fashionable high heels she had to look up to glare at Lavender. "You'll need to be."

As she strode off, Devan gestured helplessly at her friend. "You had to say that?"

"What? It's the truth. I just left out names not to dignify the guilty with attention."

Mead stepped closer. "Don't worry about it, ladies. I'm coming to the conclusion that the only time she's happy is when she's making someone squirm or sweat."

"Is that why you're here?" Devan asked. "I would think this kind of event is the last place you'd want to be." But he certainly looked like he was born to be here—and at grander functions.

"I suspect I'll end up agreeing with you. But she happened to say the magic words."

"I don't follow."

"She told me you'd be here."

Behind her, she could hear Lavender murmur, "Awww," and knew her relentlessly romantic friend was dewy-eyed and grinning. For her part, all Devan could do was feel increasing dread. "You were had. Don't look now, but she's already watching how you're staying here instead of following her."

"She changed outfits, you know."

Devan shouldn't have been surprised, but she was. Talk about having been set up…she couldn't even take any pleasure in the fact that in the end, the woman had embarrassed herself. They would end up paying for that, as well. She picked up the corsage box that Lavender had set down on a table and handed it to him. "Give this to someone who might enjoy it."

Although Mead took it, he studied her with concern. "Tell me, what I can do to help?" he asked.

Beyond him, Devan could see Pamela, in search of an ally, scornfully gesturing to the chamber's president and his wife. "Don't give us special attention."

Approximately an hour later Devan sat on the back of her SUV, parked at the end of the building, and wondered if she would be better off humbling herself to Pamela or apologizing to Lavender and moving with Blakeley to the North Pole. She did urge Lavender to go home because she'd gone above and beyond to get additional last-minute orders done for the Polk funeral.

Inside, the schedule was probably well past entertainment and the meal moving to the dessert and awards phase. She estimated that she had another thirty to forty-five minutes or so before she could return inside to take everything down. Fighting a yawn, she tugged her black suede jacket closed over her black cashmere sweater and wool slacks. It wasn't all that cold, but being tired made her particularly sensitive to the chill in the night air.

Sipping the hot cider she'd brought in a thermos, she

thought about Blakeley and hoped she was sleeping by now. Tomorrow the store would only be open a half day and she'd promised Blakeley she could come along and work like a real "helper," as the cute chatterbox put it. Jorges had approved of their idea to offer Nina the job as Lavender's assistant and when Devan had talked to the teen by phone, Nina had enthusiastically agreed to start tomorrow, too.

The auditorium door opened and someone stepped outside. The man immediately tugged at the knot of his tie. Glancing around, he spotted her and strolled over.

"Want some company?" Mead asked.

Devan sighed. "You shouldn't be out here."

"You must've guessed I could only take so much of what's going on in there." He sat beside her. "Question is, why aren't you inside? I thought I saw a sticker on the shop's door indicating you're a member."

"We are, but we knew we'd be too beat to sit through rubber chicken and the rest, never mind trying to set up everything while teetering on heels and being hampered by formal clothes."

"As much as I'd like to see you, um, 'hampered,' I like that outfit, too." He reached out and gently brushed the hair behind her right shoulder. "This is gorgeous."

His slightest touch had the most incredible effect on her and Devan could feel every cell in her body vibrate with awareness. "How am I supposed to stay exasperated with you when you say things like that?"

"You're worrying too much, lovely lady. My mother is learning that I won't be manipulated and that I'm drawn to you. She didn't say another negative word at the table."

She didn't have to; she'd already spread her displeasure

before they'd sat down to dinner. And she wasn't about to risk alienating her son there; on the contrary, she'd used it as an opportunity to show how much she adored him and delighted having him escort her. Devan couldn't bear to watch and as soon as she was convinced everything was as perfect as she could get it, she'd come outside.

"I don't remember seeing Riley Walsh," she said to change the subject.

"I'm taking his seat."

"That's the only thing that must have mollified your mother. This isn't something a political candidate can afford to miss."

"She's telling everyone that he's out of town on important business, but as fast as she changed the subject, I have a feeling she really isn't sure where he's gone."

That was odd—and troubling to Devan. "He's done that before and, come to think of it, right after he's had a hot check."

"Does his wife go with him? What's she like?" Mead asked quizzically.

"Polly…well, she's no glamour queen like your mother. You never see her and Riley together. She's very involved in her church and her children." Devan finished her cider and offered Mead some.

"I'm fine, thanks. By the way, did Walsh's check clear?"

"Apparently. I haven't gotten any more calls from Ben at the bank."

Mead glanced around. "And where's your partner?"

"Off hoping to resuscitate a relationship. She deserves the break, and taking all that down," she said, nodding inside, "goes a lot faster than putting it together."

"Is that why you're hanging around?" he asked, incredulous.

"Why else? It won't take an hour. Then I'll bring the flowers back to the store and head home myself."

"I don't like the idea of you working alone so late."

"The caterers will be cleaning up, as well. And you know the police station is only a block away from the store."

"We passed it coming here. It already looked locked down tight. I'll send my mother home with Philo and help you."

"Absolutely not," Devan replied ignoring the way her heart skipped a beat. "Right now your mother is only angry with me for not following her directives to the letter, do you want her to totally hate me?"

"My mind's made up."

"I take back what I said about you being a gentleman. You're stubborn and a bully."

"Can you change that to protective bully?"

"The most dangerous kind." But Devan couldn't help but smile.

Mead's gaze stayed riveted on her. "You're beautiful when you do that. I'll bet men lose track of what they're thinking all the time around you."

As a new wave of delicious warmth spread through her, Devan crossed her arms and toed pebbles with her boot. "Sure, and vehicles jump curbs all the time crashing through plate-glass windows when I walk by."

"It wouldn't surprise me a bit if they did."

She had to change the subject; she loved to hear people compliment Blakeley, but grew uncomfortable when it was directed at herself. "Did it bother you to be saluted prior to the national anthem being played?"

"Hell, yeah, it did. A standing ovation for failing to do my job...terrific."

"It made the old-timers feel good. You were a warrior,

Mead. Shaking your hand, hugging you, makes the veterans feel the connection between the past and the present."

"I wouldn't mind if you wanted to hug me."

Devan rolled her eyes. "That didn't take you long."

"What can I say? You have that effect on me."

Devan cleared her throat. "Did you see anyone inside that you recognized? Talk to anyone who triggered something familiar?"

"Only you."

"You're determined to keep me blushing." Devan scanned the packed parking lot, but didn't really see any of it.

"Do you have a problem with that?"

"I—no. It's nice."

"Good. We're making progress, as my therapists used to say."

"Which, the head or body ones?"

"Both. I was consistently stubborn and resisted their help for some while."

She didn't want to think of all he'd suffered. "I'm glad you changed your mind."

"Me, too. Now."

Holding her gaze, he leaned closer, and closer, until his lips brushed against hers. She returned the gentle caress, until he eased her lips apart and suckled gently on her lower lip. When it was her turn, Devan lightly scored his lower lip with her teeth. Feeling him tense, she leaned back.

"Is something wrong?"

"Hardly. Feel free to do that again. Do anything you want. As a matter of fact, why don't we crawl in here completely, shut the door and find out who can steam the windows the most?"

"If you keep looking at me that way, I'm afraid my

clothes are going to be what's steaming. Lavender is right, you're all but irresistible in a suit."

"Let's test that theory."

Devan tipped her head back to receive his next kiss. It was instantly intimate and arousing, and when Mead slid his hands into her hair, she let herself be drawn completely against him, until her breasts were pressed tight against his hard chest. His warmth was welcome, but second to his hunger; he absorbed her essence as though he'd wanted dessert after all.

When the front door opened and someone coughed discreetly, Mead reluctantly ended the kiss only to swear gruffly. He swore again when they saw Philo had come outside.

"I'll go give him the news."

"Mead…it's not necessary."

"It is to me. Don't worry."

He had to be kidding. Devan went to the front of the SUV to brush her hair and check her lipstick, then she reentered the auditorium through the side kitchen door in the hopes of a miracle and missing further misery courtesy of Pamela Regan's mouth.

"I beg your pardon?" Pamela looked dumbfounded. "Mead, this is unacceptable. Regans do not conduct themselves like common laborers. The nerve of that woman to wheedle—"

"No one wheedled." As Mead escorted his mother outside, he met the ambiguous gaze of Philo holding open the rear passenger door. "My decision. I can't imagine you could possibly feel right about a woman working alone at this hour."

"You're right, of course." Pamela turned to Philo. "You come back after you drop us off at the house and make sure she's all right."

"As you wish, ma'am."

As his mother climbed in, Mead took control of the door and shut it soundly. Then he looked directly into Philo's amused eyes and said softly. "Over my dead body."

The auditorium emptied quickly and Mead found Devan was one of the last around. Three others were back in the kitchen bagging trash and loading the dishwasher one last time. All three were men, which made him feel even better about staying behind.

She'd just finished boxing the head table coverings when he reached her. Taking the box out of her arms, he said, "Keep boxing and I'll load."

Devan paused. "I'm afraid to ask—was your mother furious?"

"Let's not mention her again tonight, okay?"

She looked like she was going to argue, but in the end, she did as he'd suggested.

They worked quietly and efficiently, and by the time they were in her truck, a spare twenty-five minutes had passed.

The unloading at Dreamscapes went as fast. "What happens to all of these?" Mead asked as they closed the cooler for the last time.

"We'll donate the cut flowers to the hospital because we can't guarantee they'll last as we advertise they will. Some we'll send over to Café on the Square. We keep them in fresh flowers in exchange for our business label being on the vases."

"Sounds like good neighboring as well as smart business."

"We think so. As for the potted chrysanthemums, we'll put most back into the nursery."

They were ready to lock up and a new emotion spread between them. Mead found her increased reticence and unwillingness to look at him a clear enough indication of what the problem was.

"Devan, relax."

"I'll take you home."

"No good. Peace of mind means making sure you're inside yours. You can let me out at your place and I'll walk to the house."

"It's getting colder and you don't need to keep going through the park after dark."

"If we're going to keep arguing about this, neither one of us will get any rest tonight." Mead reached into his pocket and pulled out a flat little phone. "Here, log in your number and take mine. I'm still learning this gizmo."

"You finally got one."

Enjoying her spontaneity as much as her pleasure, he replied, "I like knowing you might check to make sure I'm okay."

Devan hesitated and Mead knew she immediately reverted to worrying that his mother would find out. "Does she really intimidate you that much? She's not going to know," he assured her.

"Oh, Mead. Now who's naive?"

Something must have shown in his expression because seconds later they were sitting in her SUV and she was keying data into their phones.

"You are going to read the manual, right?" she asked, handing his back to him. "You're not going to be like so many men and rely on pushing buttons and experimenting?"

"I was told I could put together an M-16 and more in the dark. I'm sure that didn't happen through clumsy grope and feel."

Devan didn't speak again until they were away from the square. "You make me feel ashamed," she said at last.

He reached over and touched her thigh. "No need. I just want you to see me, not what happened. Me."

"I do. I—" She tapped her right palm repeatedly against the steering wheel. "Life is getting increasingly crowded, Mead."

"What do you mean?"

"There are two messages on my phone from my mother-in-law."

"Is Blakeley all right?"

"Yes, but it's clear she thinks …*they* think…Jay's wife is becoming a little vague. Their word is 'inconsistent.'"

"Because you're no longer his wife." Mead shifted to watch her navigate the empty streets. "You're your own person now. They don't see that."

"Or don't want to."

She pulled into her driveway, killed the engine and released her seat belt. Once out of the vehicle, they met at the walkway.

"Thank you. For everything," she told him.

"Has it struck you that we have more in common than we've been aware of?"

Keys in hand, looking dead on her feet, Devan blindly reached out to him, her hand brushing his arm, his chest. "After a twenty-hour day, I'm too sore to think."

"Open up. I know a trick that will knock you out the moment your head hits the pillow. You'll wake in the morning feeling like you've been on a week's vacation."

Mead expected her to stall or demure. To his relief, she unlocked the front door. The only other hint that she'd really run out of fuel was that she had to stand at the security keypad a moment to remember her code.

There was a light on in the dining room china hutch and one in the kitchen, supplying a soft glow to the room. As

Devan closed the door, then slid out of her jacket, Mead drank in her lithe figure. Her movements were as spare and graceful as her body, and even without his memory, he knew how different they were and that he needed to rein in his strength not to hurt her.

For a second she just looked at him and gave him a self-conscious little shrug.

He came to her and kissed her forehead gently. "Turn around." Taking hold of her shoulders, he directed her, then breathed in the floral scent of her hair as he began to massage her shoulders. "What's that shampoo?" he murmured.

"Freesia. It's a spring flower, but Blakeley and I both love it."

"Me, too." What she would never see was his frown as he felt her tense muscles. His own physical therapist would have lined him out if he'd been this tight. "You carry a lot of weight on these small shoulders."

"I'm tougher than you—oh!"

He'd slipped his hands under her hair and up her neck to use his thumbs to work out the kinks there. "Hurt?"

"Yeah, then…God, you're good."

"I had a great teacher named Isaiah back at the hospital, who was planning on becoming a sports therapist. He was almost twice my size and had intended to be a professional basketball player, but an injury cut his career short."

"Bless him—for keeping his life together, and for helping you."

Mead brushed her silky hair over her right shoulder and bent to kiss the left side of her neck. "That's sweet. You taste even sweeter." He couldn't resist another kiss, and to nibble around the diamond stud in her small pink lobe.

Sighing, Devan went completely pliable, almost swaying against him. Reaching back, she steadied herself by resting her hands against his thighs as she would a tree trunk. "Whoa. And I haven't even had anything to drink."

Mead chuckled softly. "I know the feeling." He then massaged his way down her arms, shifted his hands to her small waist and worked upward. When his fingertips brushed the outer swell of her breasts, she trembled and the honest reaction went straight to his groin. He ached to do it again, to cover her with his hands and know why this woman was so attuned to his touch.

"Mead, please…?"

"That wasn't part of the therapy."

"Please."

Closing his eyes and resting his cheek against her hair, he gave her what she asked for, and learned she was wearing a sheer lacy confection under the cashmere. "Heaven help me," he rasped. "You're beautiful."

Leaning back against him nestled her bottom perfectly against his arousal. Her breathing grew shallower. When she sought a kiss, he hungrily took her mouth and stroked his tongue against hers in the same lazy tempo that he stroked her breasts.

Murmuring something indecipherable, Devan reached back, clasping her arms around his neck.

Mead couldn't resist one more moment, thrusting hips against her once, twice…but the next move would have him sliding his hand down over her flat stomach and farther, and he knew that would be too late. Wrapping his arms like a vise around her, he buried his face against cashmere and suede.

"Dev—no more."

"Oh, jeez, not again. Mead, I'm—"

"Shh. It's all right." He pressed kisses along the side of her neck until he felt in better control of his own hunger. "Are you awake enough to lock up after me?"

"Yeah."

"Do me a favor and don't turn around until I let myself out."

"Mead...stay."

The breath he sucked in hurt. "There'd be hell to pay. She'll forgive this hour or two, not the night we'll need."

Hugging her close once more, Mead went to seek the path home...and to his future.

## Chapter Ten

"All right, Philo," Mead said upon arriving at the rear gate, "the delinquent is home. Open up. I'm in no mood to tackle the wall."

"Thank you for making it a short night, sir."

Mead waited for his mother's hired man to release the lock and draw back the gate; then he rushed him and smashed him between wrought iron and wall. If it was a reaction to anything in his past, he was left as startled as the immobilized Philo looked.

"Never speak of or make reference to Ms. Anderson again without a helluva lot more respect."

"I didn't. I do." Pryce Philo's voice broke as he squeezed out the protest. "No disrespect meant, sir. I was referring to the degree of your mother's relief once she knew you were home."

"I'll speak to my mother next."

"Yes, Mr. Regan."

After waiting to see true acceptance in his eyes, Mead stepped back. Then he gestured for Philo to precede him inside.

"Something's happened, sir?" he asked, rubbing his shoulder. "You've recovering some memory?"

"Why? Do you need to log something in a journal or make a call?" While he had no proof, Mead was increasingly convinced that his mother's butler had some training in his past that had nothing to do with announcing guests or chauffeuring the lady of the house. He just wished he had a clue whether that training was legal or not.

"Sir? Not at all. You just exhibited impressive agility and skill."

"That's what happens when you hit one raw nerve too many."

"A misstep I deeply regret."

Philo did everything but bow in his retreat. Mead paid him no more attention than he trusted him. "Is it too much to hope that my mother has turned in?"

Opening the French door, Philo stood back for Mead to enter. "By the bar, sir."

Mead stayed a good yard away on the patio. "Then this would be a good time for you to excuse yourself."

"I'll just lock up after you."

"The mental cripple is capable of locking up himself."

This time Philo did incline his head. "Good night, Mr. Regan. Again, I apologize."

Mead sighed. "Don't for a second think I'm not tempted to see you're sent packing, but I've watched you—yes, while you've watched me—and I'm willing to give you some benefit of the doubt that you're not simply the sneaky, back-stabbing suck-up you appear to be."

The impeccably dressed man appeared momentarily speechless. "If I seem only that, Mr. Regan, I should turn in my notice."

"Don't be an ass, Pryce. You're exceptional and you know it. Just modify that bloodhound nose of yours to lose my scent and figure out a way to redirect any and all interest my mother shows in Ms. Anderson elsewhere."

"If that were ever achievable, it may be impossible at this stage."

"Then consider yourself fairly warned."

Mead waited until Philo disappeared before locking up. He found his mother refilling her glass—with what he didn't care, except that he wanted her sober enough to hear him now and remember what was said in the morning.

"Shouldn't you at least wait for the official bad news from the police before you ceremoniously mourn my loss?" he asked. "Or am I overestimating my value in your life?"

Pamela stopped the glass midway to her lips, then polished off the shot anyway. "I do not understand what's going on with you, Mead, but you've managed to reach the limits of my tolerance."

"Considering your behavior this evening, I'd say you lost it long ago."

"*My* behavior? I'm not the one who abandoned his mother and embarrassed an entire table of guests in the middle of dinner by simply walking out."

"At least I showed up. It's more than your pal Walsh did."

"As I told you and repeated at the table on his behalf, he was unavoidably called out of town on business."

"Do you actually believe I or anyone else bought that?" Mead slid his hands into his trouser pockets and casually strolled around the room while observing her surreptitiously. "I happen to know all is not well with Walsh Development. Now why is a man who's done as much in the area as he has bouncing a few-thousand-dollar check? And not for the first time, I understand?"

Pamela glared at him. "How dare you spread gossip like that! I can just imagine where you heard that, too. Riley Walsh is an honorable and respected businessman— and our future mayor! It's a slur against his character to suggest he's not to be trusted because of…of some minor snafu in paperwork."

"Is that what they call it these days?"

"Riley is a busy man, and as efficient as he is, he's not in control of when title companies, banks and mortgage companies all get their documentation in order. If something got momentarily out of order for a day," she explained airily with a wave of her glass, "that's hardly cause to incite a panic.

"You tell your chatty little friend," Pamela continued, pointing at Mead, "that Riley will hear about this. Let's see how much *fun* it is to malign a professional's character when she loses one of her most profitable clients!" She uttered a brief disdainful laugh. "Considering the disaster she and that hippie-freak friend of hers made of the banquet, I wouldn't be surprised if a number of people start looking to do business elsewhere."

Mead might have worried that he'd opened a can of worms, except for the flush in his mother's cheeks and the way her eyes shifted. She almost seemed…desperate?

"You're reaching," he told her. "And not well. Why didn't Walsh simply transfer funds from one account into another? Hell, why didn't he pull the money out of his personal account to cover the problem?"

She lifted her chin. "Because it wasn't worth his time, of course. Because *she* isn't worth his time."

"Devan is worth three Riley Walshes, and if I hear that you have said or done anything to hurt her or her business," he said, lowering his head and voice, "we will talk again."

"Are you threatening me?" Pamela gasped, raising her hand to her throat.

"I'm telling you that you've been outed. You're a meddler. You like being in everyone's business, then changing it to your business. What you seem oblivious of, or simply indifferent to, is the responsibility that comes with that."

"Don't realize? If it wasn't for me, this town would still be the stale farm and ranch community that your father left behind. You don't know what I risked and sacrificed for these people."

"Without knowing how accurate you are, I know that's a dangerous, not to mention insulting, statement. But if you're right, why do the only people who approach you at functions like tonight's seem to do so because they're either afraid not to at least pretend their support, or because they have something to barter?"

Pamela managed to look wounded. "You make me sound cold-blooded."

"How about not exactly a hothouse hybrid?" he countered wryly.

"Well, let me tell you that I'm not exactly inspired by what I see in you lately, either," she replied, recovering quickly. "You've changed in the last several days, and some of your behavior has raised more than a few eyebrows. At first I couldn't get you out of the house. Now you can't wait to get away from here. Then I hear reports about you spending extravagant sums on flowers to a veritable stranger, and now you're working like one of her field hands. It's beginning to sound like you have a fixation with the woman."

Mead remained silent because she wasn't wrong and what he was increasingly feeling for Devan was personal and precious. However, his mother was neither a fool nor blind.

"Are you having an affair with Devan Anderson?"

"No."

Pamela sniffed. "So she's not a complete fool and knows to play hard to get." Putting down her glass, she clasped her hands and took a deep breath. "I forgive you your male impulses, but I want you to end it before it goes further, do you hear? There were several comments made about you tonight that I could be encouraged about. Judge Otts and Congressman Gout tell me they'll have a seat open next year in the U.S. Congress. If your health continues to improve—and if you can manage not to bring shame down upon this family—I could see to it that the four of us have a meeting."

Thunderstruck, Mead shook his head. Only five minutes earlier she'd been accusing him of shaming her. "You know what? You should take the meeting yourself. I pity Washington, but Mount Vance would sure sigh in relief."

It was almost noon on Sunday when Blakeley took her seat at the kitchen table and bounced happily as she waited for her plate of stir-fry. When the doorbell rang, she sighed.

"I hope it's not company."

"Blakeley Anderson!" Devan cried. "Of all the things to say."

"You told me I could go with Michelle to the movies, and if we have company, I won't get done in time."

"You have plenty of time, although with that selfish attitude, I'm not sure you deserve to go anywhere except to your room. Now behave," she continued, turning off the electric range. "I'll be right back."

Opening the front door, she was startled to see an almost life-size toy lion. Second's later Mead's face appeared from around the fluffy mane.

"Mead." They'd talked on the phone yesterday and she hadn't expected to see him for another day or two. "How's your mother?"

Sometime later Friday night, Pamela Regan had been admitted to Mount Vance Memorial Hospital complaining of chest pains. Mead had spent the night there waiting for news, and as of yesterday doctors were still performing tests.

"Fine. Home and plotting God knows what next," he replied sardonically.

Devan was astonished that he could be so flippant about the incident. Devan may not like the woman, but she was his mother. "I was going to call your cell number shortly. What did the tests show?"

"Absolutely nothing. She's got the heart of a thirty-year-old…or a glacier. Take your pick." He lowered the stuffed animal and shrugged. "Her blood pressure was off somewhat, but that's because she'd been drinking like a fish. Devan, don't waste your energy sympathizing. I know my mother—it was an act. She couldn't get me to toe the line one way, so she figured out another to keep me at her side."

"To the point where she'd subject herself to all those tests?" Devan found the idea irrational, and frightening.

"You're not thinking anything I haven't," Mead told her. He glanced beyond her into the house. "Is this a bad time?"

"Oh, excuse me, come in." She stepped aside to let him enter, aware of her own heart's unsteadiness. She couldn't believe how much she missed seeing him. He looked wonderful dressed in a white dress shirt, jeans and a black leather bomber jacket. Closing the door, she added, "Who's your friend?"

"Well, I seem to have a problem. I need to find a home for him."

"I see. I think." Devan pretended to give the beast a close but dubious inspection. "He looks...a handful."

"Nah." Mead leaned toward her. "Between you and me, he's a pushover. Loves little girls. But he's high-maintenance. Forever wanting his ears scratched and to be combed..."

"Ah. I happen to know of someone with lots of free time on her hands. One question, though...does he snore?"

"He calls it purring."

Chuckling, Devan led the way back to the kitchen. "Let's see what we can do for you. Blakeley...look what Mr. Regan has brought for you, do you think you can let him live in your room?"

"You're having lunch," Mead said, suddenly hesitant. "I didn't look at the time, I'm sorry."

"No problem." Devan kept her voice warm, but watched her daughter's reaction to him.

Initially, Blakeley's blue eyes widened with surprise and fear, but shortly thereafter, she dropped her gaze to the hands folded in her lap.

Aware this was a critical reunion, Devan was gentle with her little girl's feelings. "What do you think, sweetheart?"

"He's big, Mommy."

Devan nodded, aware her child was giving her a message on two fronts. "Maybe we should sit him in a chair and see how he behaves during lunch. Okay?"

Blakeley shrugged.

Biting her lower lip, Devan pulled out the chair beside her daughter and placed the lion to where its head rested on the table.

"He's gonna get in trouble," Blakeley said, looking

pleased at the prospect. "You don't like when anybody puts their head on the table."

"You're right, but he's a guest, and I guess we shouldn't correct a guest, huh?" to Mead, she gestured to the chair beside hers. "Please, sit. We're having stir-fry. Hungry?"

"I don't know if I've ever had it before, but it smells great. Are you sure there's enough?"

"Plenty."

"How come you don't know?" Blakeley asked, studying him again. "You're old. You should remember lots all the way back to when you were a little kid like me."

Devan gasped. "Oh, honey—"

"It's okay," Mead interjected, slipping off his jacket. Placing it on the back of the seat, he sat and pointed to the red scar where he no longer wore a Band-Aid. His hair was starting to grow out and it wasn't as visible as before. "See this? I was hurt and now I can only remember from when I woke up in the hospital."

"What happened, did you crash your car?"

"Mr. Regan was a soldier, darling," Devan said, setting a place for Mead. Afterward, she squeezed his shoulder.

Blakeley's eyes widened again. "Were you shot?"

"Yes, but not there. A mortar went off near me and that's when I got the head wound."

"What's a mortar?"

Devan all but groaned. "It's a weapon and causes a terrible explosion. Now that's enough questions."

"Ms. Nancy at day care says it's good I ask questions and that when I get to school teachers will say I'm en-encouraging."

"Are you sure she didn't say incorrigible?"

Mead grinned. "I think it's good to ask questions, too. I've had to ask lots of questions while I've been sick."

"Will you remember when you're all better?" Blakeley asked.

"I don't know."

"Will you remember me after you go home? I have a friend whose grandmother forgets she's visited when she goes home."

"Jillian's grandmother has Alzheimer's, Blakeley," Devan said gently as she set the wok in the middle of the table. "That's a disease. Different thing entirely."

"In other words, I'll remember very well how pretty and helpful you were to me," Mead added.

Blakeley studied him for several seconds. "Stir-fry is mostly lots of vegubbles," she informed him with her usual difficulty in enunciating the word.

"It's got chicken in there some, but it's bad if you pick out the chicken only."

Devan almost burst out laughing at the way Blakeley wagged her little index finger at Mead in the same way Devan had once rebuked her daughter. "We don't eat only chicken because the vegetables are good for us."

"Thank you for telling me," Mead said somberly. "I need good-for-you food."

Heartened, Devan brought a second bowl to the table. "I hope you like wild rice. We prefer it to the white."

"Fine. I'm told I could eat grub worms and grasshoppers if I needed to."

Blakeley giggled. "No, you wouldn't."

"Some soldiers are trained to survive in places there are no stores and restaurants, honey," Devan explained. To Mead, she murmured, "I'm glad that's behind you. Or is it?"

He met her gaze. "It is. I'm home for good." Turning back to Blakeley he asked, "What are those?"

"Chopsticks." She pointed to the set next to the silverware. "Did you forget them, too?"

"I reckon."

She tilted her head and considered him another moment. "Mommy teached me."

"Taught," Devan murmured taking her seat.

"Taught." Blakeley expertly clicked hers at him. "You need help?"

With a twinkle in his eyes, Mead replied, "Yes, please."

Devan wondered if he was pretending or really didn't remember. But soon she simply sat and watched with quiet fascination as he let her daughter do the elementary school version of chopstick etiquette. His lack of success might have sent any child into peals of laughter, but Blakeley had become somber and patient, taking her job seriously, until Mead sighed and put down the chopsticks and picked up a fork.

"I'd better use this for the rest or we'll both be eating cold food and your mom will be mad at me."

"You did okay for your first time," Blakeley told him. "You just need practice."

"Thank you. I'll ask Philo if we have any at the house."

"Who's Philo?"

"My mother's—he's like a butler and chauffeur combined. His full name is Pryce Philo."

"He has a price for a first name?"

"Well, it's spelled differently. I think he's English."

"I'm English."

"You're American," Devan replied. "English as in England in Great Britain. Remember we've looked at the globe and you learned your continents and oceans? Now eat your food, missy, or you won't be ready when Michelle comes."

Blakeley had launched several more interrogations.

Each time Devan would have to redirect her attention to her plate. Finally the child asked to be excused.

"Can I go put my lion in my room?" she asked.

"Yes, you may. Then you need to rinse out your mouth and brush your hair. And what do you say to Mr. Regan?"

"Thank you."

Blakeley grabbed up the gorgeous stuffed toy and ran for her room.

"You handled that very well," Devan told Mead.

"She's adorable. It was a treat."

"I must admit that I was worried when I first opened the door."

"I should have called first, but I was concerned that you might tell me to stay away."

His intimate tone and searching look had her tingling all over, and she self-consciously fingered the first button on her V-necked white sweater. "Where on earth did you find the toy, on a Sunday, and after all you've been through the last two days?"

"Mrs. Smiley, the cook, had it in her car. She just bought it for her grandson's nursery. I asked her if she could get another and sell this one to me. She agreed." He nodded to his empty plate. "This was excellent. Thank you."

"Did you really not know about the chopsticks?"

"Really."

Devan bit her lip, wondering how thwarting it must be to come up against so many blanks.

He covered her hand with his. "It's all right."

"No, it's not. You could be dead and I might never—" Stunned by what she was feeling and about to admit, she shot to her feet and carried her plate to the sink.

In the next instant he was behind her, his hands at her waist. "Might never what?" he asked quietly.

"I misspoke."

"No, you didn't. Please don't deny me the words. I know this is the wrong time and place, but let me at least have them."

"I was about to say have touched you again," she whispered.

"And I might never kiss you again," he replied just as softly. "I want to now. I want to press you against this cabinet and hold you in my hands. I want to turn you around and kiss you until you're all over me like a fever."

Devan sighed shakily and gripped the counter. "Stop. I've got just about enough self-control not to do just that. Please, give me a little space, Mead."

"Will you do one thing for me?"

"I can only say I'll try."

"Tell me you want me."

"Mead…is anything more obvious?"

"Say it."

She touched his cheek. "I want you."

Mead took hold of her hand and pressed a fervent kiss into her palm. "Thank you." After a second, he stepped back and said, "One more request."

Her sigh was barely audible.

"Help me remember how to drive."

## Chapter Eleven

"At the risk of sounding annoyingly redundant, do you remember anything?" As Mead studied the SUV's control panel, Devan watched him. He looked slightly hesitant and she hoped she was doing the right thing. For a moment she thought back to the chopsticks...and there was a world of difference between handling a couple of skinny sticks and driving a thousand-plus pounds of steel.

"I haven't wanted to until recently," he told her. "I watched Philo enough to sense I could get to where I needed to go if I had to. I don't know that it would be the smoothest ride, though. Or the quietest." He cast her a wry look. "This must seem nuts to you."

"Not at all."

"It's embarrassing to me."

Nodding her understanding, Devan recalled, "You did

have your vain side, Mead. I empathize because we have that in common."

"I really appreciate you letting Blakeley go to the movie with her little friend."

"I'm glad it was already planned. While I'm semiwilling to risk my own safety, I wasn't going to risk my child's."

"I wouldn't let you."

His quiet certainty won him more approval than she wanted to admit. "So get this thing started. Chatty Cathy will be home by five."

They drove out in the country to a relatively straight stretch of road she'd explained was near Jorges' family's leased mobile home. Devan had pulled onto the shoulder and they'd switched seats.

"You want to go stop by and say hello?" Mead asked, buckling his belt.

"Heavens, no. First of all, you aren't getting out of this that easily." Buckling up, too, Devan swept her hair over to fall across her right shoulder in order to watch him better. "Second, they would be mortified. Gracious, but embarrassed to be able to offer what they would gauge as so little. Also, Jorges' wife works odd jobs. If either or both of them have managed to get a few hours off, they sure don't need to spend it trying to be sociable to their employer."

Adjusting her sunglasses, she teased, "Stop dawdling, Regan…and see that you don't do anything to make me have to call my insurance agent."

Any worries she may have experienced were quickly put to rest as he started the vehicle and continued their journey without burning off any tread from her new tires or doing any heart-stopping swings into ditches or head-ons with trees.

After a few miles she said, "You realize I'm about to call you a fraud?"

"I was almost ready to do that myself."

A certain note in his voice drew her focus off the road and she realized how he was perspiring. Concerned, she thought about what was up ahead. "After this bend there's a roadside park. It'll be on your right. Pull in there."

When he spotted it and signaled, turned and came to a halt, she asked, "Are you okay?"

He used both hands to rub his face, then wiped them on his jeans. "Don't worry. It's just your run-of-the-mill anxiety attack."

"But you did it, Mead."

"Yeah, I managed to drive six miles down an East Texas road without getting ambushed by buzzards or getting blown up by a cow patty."

"Were you having a flashback?"

"No. I did feel like I was about to, though."

"Would that be a good thing, do you think?"

"Probably, I don't know. It sure didn't feel it."

Devan stroked the warm leather across his back. "The point is, you can drive."

He didn't seem as convinced. "What if I do this on a freeway?"

"So you rent a car and find out." At his startled look, she replied with a haughty one of her own that she was sure would impress his mother. "Hey, you're not ruining my upholstery."

It took him a second to catch on and then he burst into laughter. "You're tough, Teach." Rubbing his hands over his hair, he exhaled. "Okay, tantrum over."

It was the first time for her to witness the frustrations of his condition and it might have been scary witnessing it early on in a hospital, but she was proud to have been the one to help him through it today. "I wish I could get through to you how well you're doing, Mead." She spoke warmly and reached over to squeeze his hand. She couldn't imagine what it must be like to have every minute of one's life be filled with the unknown, no references or experience to guide you.

Mead took her hand and brought it to his lips. "I'm acting about Blakeley's age, aren't I?"

He sounded so disgusted with himself, Devan released her seat belt. "Come on, let's settle those jitters by walking around a bit."

Stately pines shaded the area and there were two picnic tables and trash barrels for weary travelers needing to stretch their legs and revive themselves.

"This is pleasant. Should I remember it?"

"Ho...don't ask me about where you wooed and plundered."

Choking, he massaged his chest. "Stop! I can't take any more."

While Mead wandered around, tossing a few early pinecones, Devan climbed up on the picnic table. Not one car had passed yet, but that's why she'd come this way. This was a quieter part of town and more so on the weekends.

After a few minutes Mead settled down beside her. "I'm okay now," he said.

"I'm glad." She rubbed his thigh. "Don't be hard on yourself."

"It's okay, I was just remembering how these moody episodes used to last for days. I guess I'm improving," he said, studying his loosely clasped hands as he rested his forearms on his knees.

"Looks like it to me."

"When I first came out of the coma, and those catatonic periods and everything, the doctors tried to get me to relax

and let things evolve at their own speed. I'm only beginning to get it."

"You should call and pass on the news."

"Wiseguy."

"No, I'm serious." Devan matched his position to best
watch his profile. "Walk me through it.

"Well, one minute you're fine, your mind completely
vacant, and in the next about three million questions
bombard you almost all at once, and they all carry the
weight of doubts. One thing the doctors have been wrong
about is that I didn't get any of my past back. Oh, sure, I
remembered not to put lemon slices in my coffee, but not
how to walk…how to shave, but not how to drive a car."

Devan nudged his knee with hers. "In a way, we all experience shades of that every day. The world is changing
so fast. When we wake in the morning, we don't know if
some new computer system has been developed that we'll
have to learn, two countries have changed their names,
and six have new heads of state. I'm still trying to
remember how much a postage stamp costs now, and I
just heard they're going up again. I know that must seem
minuscule compared to your experience, but add on a
full-time job, family…anyone would appreciate the stress
you've been under.

"Mead, I've only been around you a week and can tell
you've come a far way. That man in the park was ready for
a final option. He had no interest in life. You do. I think
you'll start to see even faster growth with every day."

"You're the key."

"Oh…I think this country has a bit to do with it," Devan
said, taking in the view. "It's not perfect, but it's rife with
spirit, most of it good."

Mead reached over to stroke her ring finger where only

a Band-Aid remained. "You mentioned wanting to leave once and not having the chance. Tell me what your life has been like," Mead urged. "There's such a steady certainty about you, and yet I'd think being alone with a child to raise would be intimidating for anyone."

"I'm hardly alone. Jay's parents remain very much a part of our lives. Lavender isn't just a business partner, she's...well—" she laughed "—for a wild woman, she's a devoted friend and we're close. And I have my faith, a precious child, a chance to do what I love—being outdoors." She shrugged. "I'm content and grateful."

"But I've seen you upset about the way your in-laws have...what? Constrained your life."

"I told you it's not perfect. That doesn't mean we don't find things we can agree on. You know the terrible shape the auditorium is in? Connie is a member of the Civic Club that does fund-raisers to work toward replacing it with something suitable for today's music and theater productions. And Jerrold, for all of his conservative ideas about a woman's place, is a painstaking volunteer at the military cemetery in town where he frequently can be seen walking the aisles teary."

"I guess I'm beating around the bush," Mead said, "and really want to ask if Jay's absence still hurts?"

Devan was glad he'd brought up the subject. "My sadness is for my daughter. I know what it's like to grow up without much of a father figure. A grandfather helps— he'll teach you to fish and introduce you to songs and singers you won't appreciate until you're his age. But a father—mind you I don't say 'daddy' like the rest of the sisterhood—teaches you...I don't know. Maybe that it's okay to walk alone, to recognize when to stick something out for the long haul, and when to cut and run?"

"Anytime you get the urge to talk in the future," Mead murmured, "I'm here for you."

In self-defense Devan allowed that maybe they were getting too serious. It was a beautiful autumn day, one waning. It was time to give him another chance to firm up his skills behind the wheel. "There's a prospect," she chuckled. "You, the man who stops my brain like an unwound clock as soon as you look at me."

And did once more.

She sensed him leaning toward her seconds before it happened and, contrary to her intentions, met him with the yearning of the lost. Sunlight seeped through the pines gilding the moment, but not with tender nostalgia.

"Come on."

Dazed, Devan followed as he took her by the hand and led her back to the SUV. Had she been wrong? Had he mined a restraint she'd willingly abandoned?

As soon as he climbed in beside her, he shoved back the driver's seat as far as it could go, pulled her onto his lap and into his arms as if she were his first and only birthday present. Burying his hands in her hair, he started reminding her why he required a rulebook of his own, one with all the pages blank.

Like their last time, their first time, and the stolen moments since, everything vanished but them. In this confining steel-and-leather nest, the restrictions on taste and touch reduced them to devouring kisses and desperate caresses.

"I know," he said, racing his lips down her throat. He hurried one of her hands down to his chest. "My heart's beating as hard as yours. My skin is as hot. Touch me."

She made short work of the shirt buttons. Slipping her hand inside and splaying her fingers, she explored the mat of hair covering his chest, his nipple already pebble-hard. She made it harder by wetting her finger and stroking him again.

Mead moaned and nipped at her neck, rocked his hips beneath her. Reaching between them, he unbuttoned her sweater. His touch affected her as much as the cooler air and she arched upward toward his heat, toward him.

"I'm cold. Warm me."

"Let me see," he rasped instead. His fingers brushed against the nude-colored lace of her bra. "That's beautiful."

So was the way he slipped down the lace and lifted her into his hand, the exquisite torment of his thumb against her taut nipple. "Mead...your mouth."

She barely got the words out before he was doing exactly what she wanted, wetting her, stroking her with his tongue, suckling to bring her deeper into his heat. At first she watched, captivated by the erotic sight, but it was too good and she closed her eyes and clasped his head to lose herself in the moment.

And still it wasn't enough. Their inability to keep from rocking and writhing against each other soon had Mead sliding his hand between her thighs. When she cried out and bucked against him, he pulled away only to slide his hand into the waistband of her jeans.

"Kiss me," he demanded gruffly. When he found the hot, wet silk between her legs, she held him there by tightening her thighs, but there was no stopping the tremors already starting. "Let me feel it happen," he coaxed, seeking her breast again. "Come for me."

She didn't have a choice. His large hands, so often gentle, grew bolder and invasive fingers stole the rest of her control. When it began happening, she could only give herself to it and him.

Her breathing had just begun stabilizing when a pickup

of teens raced by. Lying across Mead, she couldn't see them, but boys were boys and they hooted and honked as they sped by.

Mead groaned and reluctantly straightened her clothes. "Thanks for the hard landing, boys," he muttered. But he didn't let her sit up until she was decent and no one else was around who might recognize her. "Are you okay?"

"Yes, but you're not." After a slight pause she made a decision. "I could call and ask if Blakeley can stay for dinner."

Framing her cheek with his hand, Mead kissed her, exposing all of his hunger. "When we get to bed, an hour isn't going to be enough, Devan. I'm going to want all night with you. Nothing less."

Nothing less. It was a promise she didn't have to verbalize. It had been in her heart for days.

## *Chapter Twelve*

"Did you hear me?"

Jarred out of her daydream, Devan blinked at Lavender standing across the workstation table at Dreamscapes. The instant their eyes met, Lavender burst into chortling laughter and her jewelry jingled cheerfully as she applauded.

"Well...*well.* Didn't someone have a particularly fine Sunday."

Devan's first impulse was to blush; her second was to swat at her friend's backside with her clipboard. She went with the second. "Mostly wishful thinking and if you repeat that anywhere, you'd better hope your will is in order."

"No disrespect meant, sweetie. I knew the way his eyes were gobbling you up at the banquet that he would be in touch. Dare I hope he did more than touch?"

Afraid that Nina would walk in at any moment, Devan

glanced toward the nursery door where she would invariably appear. "I am not sleeping with him."

"Yeah, well, you're thinking about it, don't try to sell me otherwise. And all I care is that you don't get disappointed or hurt. The rest, I understand, you're right. It's none of my business and I can behave—ha! Somewhat. But not if you were hurt."

Devan's annoyance melted in a flash. "Okay, okay. I'm sorry for snapping at you. I'm just not ready to be juggling a relationship when we're in the midst of a business crisis."

"I hear that, but we've gotta take what we can get while the opportunities present themselves." Lavender poured them both a mug of steaming raspberry tea. "Next thing you know young Blake'll be graduating from high school and you'll be dealing with cottage cheese butt."

"Thank you for the vivid visuals, and the confidence." But Devan accepted the mug with a reluctant grin. She'd left the house without any caffeine or anything else hot to avoid traffic due to the weather and to get Blakeley safely to day care.

"That doesn't answer my question, dear friend."

"I'm fine." She patted Lavender's back in thanks, aware how tender the woman's heart was despite her extroverted personality. "Yes, I had been thinking of him. Yes, he came over, but things didn't go to the extent you think."

"Something happened."

Disgusted that her face apparently gave away so much where Mead was concerned, Devan put down her mug and ducked her head to braid her ponytail. The way it was raining she'd be a drowned rat by the time today was done even wearing a rain poncho. "This is fragile."

"Yeah. I can see that." Lavender dropped her usual every-day's-a-party persona and frowned. "I want you to be happy."

"I'm happy. My life is blessed. This is…could be more."

Lavender breathed a reverential, "Wow."

Securing the braid with a rubber band, Devan managed a tolerant smile. Even when Lavender had gotten lost in a relationship to the detriment of the business, there was no way she could get too upset with her. Considering all the Rileys and Pamelas in the world, it needed the 24k romantics.

"You didn't know him before," she told her. "He was something, but…this is a different man from the one who'd lived in that body."

"It's a bit battered, but sexy body."

"He was before, too. You just couldn't tell if he was running from something or to it."

"Does he know now?"

"Maybe we both do."

"That is *very* sexy."

Devan nodded.

"So you're…gonna kinda date?"

"We're kinda headed toward a blowout affair."

"That's hot."

"Except that it will put us—as in you and me—higher on his mother's hate list." She didn't want to worry Lavender prematurely, but she kept getting the feeling that Pamela was considering financing her own florist, maybe a landscaping business, too. It would be a sure way to benefit from Riley in yet another manner. Either way she expected at any moment to be told they no longer had the lawn care service account for Regan Mansion.

"You'll need to strategize," Lavender said, breaking into

her thoughts. "Drink your tea before it gets cold, hon, I'm good at this. You can meet out of town. I can cover for you."

"That's not his way, or mine, which means if it happens, I have to deal with Jay's parents, too."

Lavender had met Connie and Jerrold once and had avoided them ever since. She said she thought she'd met things with more life in them in the fresh produce aisle at the market.

"I wish they'd take a long cruise or something and quit sucking the life out of you," she told Devan. "It would do them good to broaden their perspective."

"It's not their fault that they see the world differently. And you know they've been a big help when you're in a scheduling bind."

"First things first," Lavender said, ignoring Devan. "How's Blakeley? Has she had any contact with him since…?"

"Yesterday. It worried me at first—he just showed up— but he brought her the neatest life-size lion." Blakeley had named the thing Crumbcake because of the way it smelled. Apparently the Regans' cook baked a good deal and the scent permeated everything including her car.

"Well, he can afford it."

"I think the toy was overly generous as it was, but maybe you were thinking it should have been something in the category of a child-size BMW?"

"Busted again. I never can keep my opinions to myself. Blame it on my folks, Dev. They thought toe rings and shoelaces were as good as designer sandals."

Trying not to laugh, Devan finished her tea and rinsed her cup. "I just don't want Blakeley to think she deserves a present every time she sees him."

"With that responsible head on your shoulders, you won't let that kid of yours get too spoiled."

"Thanks." Checking her watch, she wondered what was keeping Jorges and the crew. "Did Nina call or say they'd be late this morning?"

"No, but some roads are already flooded. Could be they'll have to take the long way around." Lavender nodded to the display cooler. "Speaking of, take a look at her first effort."

Devan did and grinned at the colorful arrangement. "It's darling."

"It looks like it exploded from a piñata. Thank goodness it's for another teenager."

"It reminds me of the shawl her mother crocheted for your birthday."

"Can you handle two of us who love color?"

"Just pray pastels don't become all the rage again." Devan collected her paperwork, grimacing over the first work-order. "We'll be at the last Walsh home in Manor Estates for most of this week whether it keeps raining or not. Mercy, this is a big one."

"Don't forget the Halloween displays for the Saunders and Templetons."

That got Devan's attention. "What?"

Lavender backed out of the storage cooler, holding a big container loaded with the chrysanthemums to be prepared for the café. "You didn't see my note? They called one right after the other. I left it on the counter."

"When?" Devan began flipping through papers.

"Wednesday—no, Tuesday."

It did no good to try to remember. Devan knew she was guilty of male preoccupation, something she'd complained to Lavender about when she'd become infatuated and messed up. "We can't do it. I'm sorry. I accept responsibility, but we're booked solid."

"They put down a hefty deposit, Dev."

Therefore, somehow she needed to pull off a miracle. This was one time she wished Mead would walk through the door, but he'd told her he would have to escort his mother to the hospital for a last checkup, regardless of the sham he suspected, and then had things he needed to do.

"Have they called complaining yet?"

"No, but my gut says they will this morning."

They were nice people and didn't deserve to be disappointed because of her ineptitude. Somehow…somehow…

"Oh, help." Lavender had gone to the front counter to double-check herself and suddenly held up a sheet of paper. "It got stuck between some of my stuff. Hon, I'm sorry." Lavender looked almost as defeated as Devan felt.

"Hey, it happens. At least I don't have to phone them and ask what it was they'd wanted." She read the orders and mentally figured what she would have to do. "Tell you what…Jorges and his guys can deliver the shrubbery, the arbor material and the tiered water fountain. Since they can't plant, and they can't lay the concrete for the arbor posts, the fountain should be what they focus on. While they're doing that, I'll take Enrique and Pasquale with me to the Saunders'. They sure can't do grass. If the Templetons call, tell them I'll have theirs done by this evening."

"Are you sure? As bad as conditions are, you'll do good not to catch pneumonia, never mind trigger your throat thingy again."

"This being Texas, with luck this will all change to snow and we can buy ourselves a day."

"Don't even joke about that." Lavender shuddered. "Have you forgotten the last time it snowed and we lost electricity for hours?"

True. The only reason they'd saved the tropicals was that Devan had brought a kerosene heater from home.

"Snow request withdrawn," she said, scooping up her things. "And I'm gone."

"Hey!" Lavender called behind her. "Don't forget to call Connie."

"Oh, jeez. Blakeley. Poor baby, and she so hoped to sleep in her own bed tonight. I'll do it. Thanks. Hi, Nina. 'Bye, Nina," she sang, ducking through the back door as the girl entered.

About thirty minutes later Devan was sighing over not being able to reach Connie by phone as she followed the Dreamscapes van into the estates. They were about to turn into the next street when a new model bronze-colored Dodge pickup flashed its lights at her. She didn't realize it was Riley until she lowered her window.

"Hey, sugar. Get a load of the new wheels."

Only Riley could pay his debts with hot checks and yet think nothing of trading in his one-year-old leased pickup for a newer model. To add injury to the insult, the rain was blowing in on her side. "I'll be real happy for you, Riley, if you tell me you've also picked six good numbers in the lottery."

He pretended her stale joke was hilarious. "I'm working on it. Listen, I just came from the hacienda for a final inspection before closing this afternoon. You did a fine job, so I'm telling my girl to release payment to you."

Devan wondered how Joellen stood working for the man, let alone being called his "girl" instead of secretary? "Should I check on available funds before depositing it?"

"Aw, I don't blame you for being a bit sore. But you just pop that thing into your account and we'll be caught up, right?"

"If you really want to make me feel better, you can

include a deposit on the work we're about to start on that Mediterranean villa on the circle."

"You deserve it. Proud to do business with you." Winking at her, he moved on.

"Well, he was in a fine mood," she said to herself as she closed her window and continued on her way. Maybe he had resolved whatever financial trouble he'd been having. Maybe that business trip turned out to be good news after all.

Deciding she'd pass the news on to Lavender as soon as she got hold of Connie, she keyed the Andersons' number in the phone's directory. This time her mother-in-law answered.

After listening to Devan explain her latest plight, Connie replied, "Dad and I had plans, dear. It's our dinner-and-a-movie night."

"Oh. Where are you going and what are you going to see?"

"Nowhere. What I mean is, I get takeout and he picks up a movie at the video store on his way home." Connie lowered her voice as though someone might be eavesdropping on their conversation. "It's part of our church's marriage counseling course we started to strengthen marriages."

"Well, that's an interesting idea," Devan said, pulling into the driveway behind the van. "Although I always thought you and Dad had a perfectly fine relationship."

"Oh, we do," Connie replied quickly. "But our minister recommended it to the entire congregation and Dad agreed."

And whatever *Dad* decided became law, Devan thought. She didn't mean to feel so cynical, but it still stung that they disapproved of how she was living her life and raising her daughter. "Okay, well, enjoy then. I'll talk to Lavender. I'm sure she can keep her until—"

"Wait! We'll reschedule to tomorrow."

"No, don't do that," Devan replied, a little surprised at her hasty reversal after taking pains to explain herself. "You help out plenty as it is. Blakeley adores Lavender and she—"

"Devan, no!" After her sharp interjection, Connie hesitated. "Dad—I mean, we would prefer Blakeley doesn't spend too much time in Ms. Smart's house. It's not appropriate, especially considering her living arrangements."

Had she heard correctly? "Rhys is a police officer, and they're no more likely to do anything in front of Blakeley than you are."

"Please, Devan. I've told you our feelings about this, now please respect them. I know Jay would agree."

She almost snapped back, "Jay is dead!" But that would only upset her mother-in-law further. Devan could see it was time to sit down with her in-laws and have a serious talk. If they were this judgmental of Lavender, how could they possibly accept her having a relationship with Mead? They needed to resolve the issue before the small chasm that was evolving between them grew into something irreparable. Unfortunately, that conversation would have to wait until she got her schedule under control again.

"All right," she said politely. "Thank you, and tell Blakeley that I'll call her later."

As Devan disconnected, she realized her hand was shaking.

It was almost nine o' clock when Devan finished the Templetons' yard. It had taken her longer because she'd insisted on Enrique catching a ride home with Jorges and the others and she'd tackled the job herself. Adding minutes to the clock had been the Templetons themselves running outside with umbrellas and raincoats over their heads to view the sprawling display of hay bales, dozens of pumpkins and gourds, a family of four scarecrows representative of the Templetons, and numerous pots of chrysanthemums. Devan barely remembered what she'd said as they'd repeatedly thanked her.

Several minutes later she returned to the shop to leave the paperwork so Lavender could bill them and the Saunders for the balance they owed first thing in the morning. Her penmanship was so off—she hoped her friend could read her writing. It had continued to rain all day and it was pouring again. Drenched to her skin, Devan had turned the SUV's heater on maximum and the blowers all directed at her, but she remained bone-cold. She knew it was due to mental fatigue as much as physical, and as she locked up, she hoped she could hold it together long enough to get home and jump into a steaming shower.

She was feeling considerably sorry for herself and ready to curse the suddenly stubborn door lock when vehicle lights illuminated her. Peering through the rain, she hoped it was whichever officer had night duty tonight. When she saw it was a truck and that it was pulling in behind her vehicle, she suffered several spasms of dread. Was she in danger? Surely she couldn't be punished with another visit from Riley....

Ready to key the horn alarm on the SUV and fumbling for her cell phone to call 911, she saw the driver's door open and someone rush out and run toward her.

"It's me, Devan!"

Relief and exhaustion took their toll, and she started to cry. Call it the last straw, a bad scare, but it was enough to reduce her to a trembling, blubbering wreck.

"Oh, damn, sweetheart," Mead said, crushing her against him. "I tried to holler fast enough so you wouldn't get spooked."

"I kn-know."

"You're working so late. I figured you were, and that was worrisome enough, but then I started imagining something had happened."

"No. Yes. I mean, I'm just…" Devan couldn't continue and just gripped fistfuls of his leather jacket. It was going to get ruined in the rain, she thought inanely.

Mead lowered his head until his warm lips and breath caressed her right ear. "I'm here, baby."

"Why?"

"Why am I here? Isn't it obvious? I've been looking for you. I got my license renewed and then I bought a truck. After that I came looking for you, but I got lost."

"Oh, Mead."

"Well, turned around a little."

"Why didn't you call?"

"It was damned near impossible this morning while getting my mother through with her appointment."

Pamela. Devan summoned the grace to ask, "I'm sorry. How did that go?"

"Exactly as I expected it would. The doctor increased her blood pressure prescription and sent her home. She tore that to shreds in the car and had Philo drive her to Dallas. She said since it was obvious she was going to die due to the incompetence of doctors that she needed to meet with her lawyer to make sure her estate is in order."

So the woman was a hypochondriac as well as a manipulative witch. The only reason Devan was sorry was for Mead not to have the loving family he deserved. She sighed. "I wish you would have called after she left."

"I should have. But I wanted to surprise you."

He did that.

"Come on. Let's get you home," he said, leading her back out into the rain toward the SUV. "We can talk tomorrow. Are you sure you can drive?"

"Yeah," she replied, although she wouldn't have bet a nickel on it. If he wasn't all but carrying her to her vehicle, her trembling legs might not have held up.

"I'll be right behind you."

She supposed the SUV drove itself home, or her brain had switched to automatic pilot for survival. At the house, she eyed his silver truck as he pulled in beside her.

"I'm sorry for not saying anything before," she told him when he came to help her out. "It's pretty."

"Pretty?" he scoffed teasingly. Mead took her shoulder bag and keys from her and checked to make sure the remote had locked up. "It's supposed to be whatever the equivalent of macho is these days."

"You had no trouble with the license?"

"Not a bit."

"Your mother was okay with you wanting a truck? She called the dealership?"

At the front door, Mead leaned her against the brick wall to unlock the door. His expression was wry. "Devan, I told you, I have my own money. I used to work for a living, you know."

"Oh. Sure."

Inside she started to head for her bedroom when Mead caught her and led her back. "Alarm."

In the dim light from the china hutch and kitchen, she peered at the keypad and pressed in Blakeley's birth year. Otherwise, it was a relief not to have too much light. Only her eyes hurt, though everything else was numb.

After locking up, Mead set her things on the carpet runner along with her poncho, so it could all drip dry, then he slipped a steadying arm around her again and led her down the hallway.

"This one," she said, barely motioning to the master bedroom. "But I'm so hungry. Let me—"

"I'll bet you never had dinner."

Or lunch. Devan dimly guessed she was better off not telling him that.

"Damn. While you're showering, I'll see what's in your refrigerator."

Mead turned on the bedside lamp and Devan winced even though the bulb wattage was low and the shade a rich burgundy. After several seconds, she realized he'd left her to undress in privacy and have her shower.

She got as far as the throw carpet between the vanity and the stall. It was a plush teal and seeing her soaked and filthy athletic shoes on it pulled a sound of dismay from her. What a mess. She didn't want to think about the trail of dirt she'd made through the house, or the equally grueling schedule awaiting her tomorrow. Not that her mind would cooperate. She was physically and emotionally spent, and even the task of undressing seemed beyond her.

Sighing, she sank to the carpet and wrestled off her shoes. Then she leaned back against the shower door and closed her eyes. Just for a minute, she thought. Just until the room stopped vibrating and spinning like the worst of amusement park rides.

## Chapter Thirteen

When Mead returned to the bedroom carrying the mug of chicken vegetable soup, two things triggered an internal alarm—Devan wasn't in bed yet, and the only running water he could hear was the pouring rain outside. Fearing the worst, he set the mug on the table beside the queen-size bed and hurried to the bathroom.

In the glow of the night-light, he saw her on the floor and for an instant a metal claw fought him for his heart. Dropping to his knees, his hand shook as he instinctively touched the side of her neck to seek a pulse.

"Devan—" Feeling the proof of her own heartbeat as well as the subtle trembling of her entire body, Mead swallowed a moan of relief. "Devan, wake up. Open your eyes. You're starting to scare me."

On his way to the kitchen he'd located and adjusted the heater's register and it was getting warmer in here, but her skin remained disturbingly cool and clammy. She needed help and fast. Shoving her shoes out of his way, he sat her up to ease her out of the denim jacket she'd been wearing beneath the poncho.

Devan moaned.

"It'll be better soon," he murmured. Even if it killed him. "It'll be warmer soon."

Briefly returning to the bedroom, he turned down the elegant wine-and-gold patchwork comforter, then stripped down to his briefs. Back in the bathroom, he turned on the shower faucets, adjusting the water to the maximum he thought she could tolerate.

Lifting Devan to her feet, he braced her against the fiberglass edge of the stall. "Hot water soon, sweetheart." Mead made short work of unbuttoning her blue corduroy shirt. Beneath that was a paler blue turtleneck, which was every bit as wet. While easing that over her head, her hair came undone. It was just as well. "I doubt even in your condition you could sleep well keeping it braided."

He'd hoped that talking to her would help stir her out of her stupor. He was an expert at getting lost in a trance state and hated that she'd pushed herself to that. It was a relief to see that as he released the fastenings on her jeans and slid them, along with her panties, down, she actually groped with the back clasps of her bra. A relief and sheer torture.

Hell, he groaned inwardly, who was he kidding, thinking he could keep this clinical? Stilling her hands, he kissed each, murmuring, "I've got it, angel."

As Mead removed that last scrap of clothing, he knew torture was an understatement. Not even goose bumps could eclipse that she was lovely and lovingly formed. "Now let's get you in there."

His voice sounded slurred to his own ears, and there was

nothing he could do to hide that he had been in a state of arousal from the moment he'd lifted her to her feet. The caress of steam didn't help...the sensual bite of water didn't, either, but none of it compared to what she did to him.

So cold, so miserable, she stood in the middle of the stall where he'd put her, her head bowed, arms crossed, hands fisted...she was the image of self-containment. No more, he thought. Mead wanted her to reach for him, to need him.

"What's it going to take?" His question was to himself as much as her.

On one of the two seats he saw a tray of bottles. The deep pink one reminded him of her bedding, so he reached for it. As soon as he poured some of the thick liquid into his hand, he knew that he'd chosen well; her hair, even her skin, had carried the alluring floral scent each time he'd been close to her.

He began with her hair, building up fragrant lather while massaging her scalp. Massages had first been torment long before they became escape for him, and he sensed as he moved down to her neck that he needed to be extra gentle with her. Easing his touch and lengthening the rhythmic, circular strokes, he worked the spasms from the tight muscles and tendons inch by inch until he came to the curve of her shoulders, then her wrists, then her fingers.

It seemed an eternity, and came so softly if he hadn't been attuned to her mood and listening, he would have missed it. But finally, he heard her exhale with appreciation, not shaky relief, when he stopped.

Pouring more soap, he continued, next her flawless back, her waist, her tantalizing bottom he already knew fit perfectly in his hands. He proved it again, this time winning a different sound from her, one that told him he was beginning to win her back from the cold and the emptiness that had been her night. Craving that sound again, he followed the trickling trailing of the water down the slope of slender hips and trim thighs and then startled her by stroking her inside where she was even sleeker.

"Mead." Wavering, Devan braced her hands against the wall.

"Welcome back, sleeping beauty. Now I know how to get your attention when you try to slip away from me."

"You have all along."

Her voice fit in this fantasy, like a dream approaching from far away. Heartening and yet agonizing for the one who waited. She had yet to accept that he had survived his tour of hell for a reason, despite not remembering why. It was her. It was *this,* his commitment to keep her from losing herself tonight. The cost would be several small deaths. As he made her tremble again, this time with awareness, not cold, Mead figured he'd endured two already.

"One day soon," he murmured as he turned her around and licked droplets from those cascading off her delicate collarbone, "we're going to do this when you can keep your eyes open and appreciate what you do to me."

A flutter of lashes and she managed to lift her lids slightly. "I can…and do."

Willing her to hold his gaze, he slid his lathered hands downward to her glistening breasts, imprinting each fingertip and then his palms with the kiss of her exquisitely taut nipples. Only his mouth could make them harder.

Devan sucked in a sharper breath before moaning softly and swaying toward him. Too human to refuse the gift and no martyr to deny it, Mead pulled her completely against him and drank that moan and then another. With his lips, teeth and tongue, he did to her mouth what his hands continued to do with her body, until her hands were no longer fisted but clutching him.

As his fingers finally broached the silky golden nest of curls, Devan surprised him. Before he could stop her, she slid his briefs from his hips. Drenched, their weight took them to the base of the stall, stealing his only physical protection from himself. When her small but strong hands closed around him, he faced a third small death.

Thrusting against her once, he drew her hand away and lightly bit the edge of her palm. "Not tonight, my precious. Even if tonight wasn't all about you, I'm not prepared."

"It's all right. My doctor keeps me on pills. Please, Mead."

But she rested her head against his shoulder as if it was too heavy for her. It was all the reminder Mead needed to fight the temptation of her sweet offer. And yet he understood that he'd done his work too well. She did need him.

"I want you to say that again tomorrow, or the next day," he said, soothing her with soft strokes and softer kisses. "Say it when you have the strength to know all I want from you." Gently leaning her back against the wall, he bent to lick the moisture from her breast. "Strength to give it to me."

He followed the path of the pounding spray resisting the hands that tried to draw him back. When he kneeled in front of her, he rubbed his face gently against her abdomen, mindful of his whiskers and her tender skin. "In the meantime…" He continued stroking her thighs and then cupping her hips. "In the meantime—" he scored one thigh and then the other with love bites "—take mine."

His name became a gasp when he turned his head and sought her essence. He showed her with his most intimate kiss all the pleasure she'd brought him so far, and all he was yearning for in their future.

When she peaked, her cry drew him to his feet and he enfolded her in his arms and held her shuddering body tightly against his. Her hips couldn't stop writhing as a powerful climax raced through every part of her being. Needing to experience at least a portion of that, Mead thrust himself between her sleek thighs and matched her sensual rocking. Then he slid his fingers deeply into her sensitive core, and this time when she peaked, they drank each other's groan of release.

As soon as he toweled them both dry, Mead carried her to the bed. If he'd considered leaving her before, it had ceased to be an option. He wouldn't get any sleep at the house anyway worrying if she was all right.

Climbing in after her, he drew her back against him. She was asleep even as he kissed her shoulder and murmured, "Dream of us."

Devan woke in the midst of another erotic dream. She'd always had sensual dreams, but after that one night with Mead they'd taken on a reality and passion that left her gasping and aching. During her marriage she'd been so ashamed and afraid she might say Mead's name out loud in her sleep, she'd tried everything from extra exercise before bed to thinking of a particularly serious story she'd heard about or read in the news to repress her subconscious. But since Jay's passing, they'd returned with a vengeance and this one just now—

Realizing she wasn't alone in the bed, Devan twisted around and met Mead's dark gaze.

Was she still caught in the dream? He was raised up on one elbow and in the dim light seeping around the blinds from the streetlamp, she saw he was naked from the waist up. That's when she realized she was naked, too.

"That was some dream." He brushed a strand of still-damp hair from her forehead. "The power of suggestion is an amazing thing. How do you feel?"

"Naked."

He smiled. "Besides that."

Slowly it came back to her…the miserably long day…her exhaustion…and Mead there when she most needed him. "Better, thanks to you."

"You may not say that in the morning when you see your hair."

She groaned. "Bad?"

"Not at all. Different than how you usually wear it. Now it's definitely a…wanton look."

That certainly went with her dream. "Did you get any sleep? What time is it?"

Without thinking she half sat up and turned around to check the clock on the bedside table. Seeing it was past two, she turned back to Mead. His expression had her heart skipping beats and her nipples responding to more than the cooler air. She knew if she reached under the blanket, she would find him hard and throbbing. Just the thought had her remembering her dream again, how he'd provoked her with his body and dark words until she took control and drove them both wild.

"What time is it?" he asked gruffly.

"I'll show you," she said, inching closer. Lowering her head, she licked his nipple, winning a low throaty murmur from him. He stroked her hair then coaxed her head up to study her in the darkness.

"You remember."

She did reach under the covers this time until her fingertips caressed him. "I want you inside me this time."

"You'll have me or I'll die trying. Come here, my dream."

As he rolled onto his back, he took her with him, sliding her up and over his body and making her totally familiar again with his size and strength despite what he'd been through. Devan shivered as his powerful legs stroked against hers. She relished how his chest rose and fell when she brushed her breasts against him to sensitize herself even more. She arched as his hands moved possessively and reverently over her.

"I hope I can last long enough to make it good for you," he said. "I don't know how durable I am…and heaven knows I don't remember what you like."

"Everything you want to do to me."

He began by gripping her waist and lifting her even higher until her breasts were level with his mouth. Closing his mouth over one, he claimed the other with his hand, initiating a dual assault on her senses.

Devan murmured with pleasure and rolled her hips against him. The heat he was creating with his mouth streaked straight through her and pooled in her womb. She remembered he'd expected nothing more from her than to accept his passion. When she'd shown that her own matched his, he'd given her an intensive education as to what turned him on, and an extensive tour of his body. She knew it as well as her own. Except for the new scars.

When her fingers lingered over a particularly large section of scar tissue near his hip, tears burned her eyes. He could have come back to her in so many different ways, she realized again. Even worse. Or not at all.

Mead took hold of her wrist and brought her hand to his lips for another of those speaking caresses that said volumes more than words. "It's over."

She blinked away the moisture from her eyes. "No, it's not. It's a part of you. They took so much already, own that, too. I've been making that mistake myself, hiding all that I am, what gave me the desire as well as the strength to go on."

"I want that woman, too," he murmured.

"She's here because you're here." Sitting up, Devan straddled him. "And I'll give you back the man I knew."

Although Mead's eyes devoured her, he immediately started to shake his head. "I've heard enough about him to know he was a fool."

Devan wrapped her arms around his neck as she sat on his lap and grazed his jawline with her teeth, spread hot, moist kisses along his neck. "He was my fantasy. Fierce, brave, independent, but I was the one he surrendered himself to. He showed me why it felt so good to him if I did this." She rose on her knees again, only to descend slightly until she felt him moist and hot, seeking her. "And when I did this—" slowly, slowly, she lowered herself onto him "—he wanted my tongue against his the same way."

Their double mating had the desired effect on Mead. As she coaxed him to lose control with her mouth, he gripped her hips and pressed deeper into her. She took all of him and relished in her power to make his entire body as taut as the part of him inside her, and understood completely as she rode him why he filled his hands with her hair and turned their kiss into a wild chase for what was still out of reach.

"Soon." The promise was a whisper as she drew back from the temptation of his mouth and, like an exotic dancer, leaned back, back until she lay against the covers like an offering on an altar.

Mead's eyes narrowed with a barely contained hunger. With hands splayed wide, he stroked her from shoulders to thigh, he took hold of her hips and ground her over him all the while watching the radiant smile lighting her face. She drove him to go faster, harder. And when he used his thumb to find and caress that nub just above where he was buried so deeply, she bucked and ecstasy consumed her.

Something close to a growl burst from Mead's lips. In a heartbeat, he was looming above her, driving into her and rasping her name as though it was the only word he knew.

Devan wrapped herself completely around him and prayed she need never let him go.

Mead returned to another time. Strapped to a bed in a room too bright for his burned eyes, his head was being split apart by metal claws. He screamed, he wept and he prayed...prayed for a face, for a touch, for a name he couldn't summon. For release from his agonizing hell.

He wanted to die, and he was. Just not fast enough.

*No...don't. Come back to me.*

The sweetest voice entreated him. The tenderest caresses lured him away from the shadow of death. He reached for the presence, but she slipped through his fingers. Yet from despair grew pleasure. Everywhere she touched him, she took away the pain. Gently, lovingly, she drew him from the nightmare.

Mead moaned and briefly opened his eyes to find it still dark, but the old panic of waking to the terror of nothingness didn't come. He could and did conjure a face, and just that filled him with a joy so deep it almost hurt, too.

*Devan.*

His body still throbbed from the ecstasy she'd brought to him. No, *was* bringing him.

This time when Mead opened his eyes, it was to the incredible intimacy of seeing and feeling Devan loving him, her hair spilling across both of his thighs. Groaning against a twisting hunger and bursting need, he gripped at the rumpled bed sheets.

"Devan," he rasped. In that instant, he knew he would die

saying her name, and as his body surged then shook from
his climax, he blindly dragged her up and into his arms.

No one and nothing, he vowed, must dare to come
between them again.

## *Chapter Fourteen*

For obvious reasons, Mead didn't check his new cell phone for messages until he left Devan. On the way back to the house, he discovered there were six—all from his mother and of an emotional range that would have raised anyone's eyebrows. As a result, he wasn't surprised when her Cadillac pulled through the electronic gates only moments behind him. It wasn't yet eight o'clock, and her mother hen-like rush to get back here would have been amusing considering her deathbed melodramatics. Offsetting that was the likelihood that some showdown was imminent.

He watched Philo park the glistening sedan by the front walkway most convenient to the right passenger door, and thought again at how odd it was that the windows weren't tinted. But then, his mother wanted to be seen being chauffeured more than she wanted privacy, thought of security or cared about UV-ray protection.

Before Philo could shut off the engine, she was out of the car and striding toward him, and Mead took special interest in her attire. As a rule, she didn't leave the master bedroom without full makeup and coordinated, designer outfit. This morning beneath an unbuttoned raincoat, she wore plain slacks, a knit tunic sweater and, more startling, a black hat over a scarf tied gypsy-style. It made him wonder if behind those oversize sunglasses, she'd bothered with eye makeup in her rush to get home.

"I've heard about lawyers being expensive," Mead drawled, figuring he might as well dive right into the emotional stew. "But I didn't know they'd be willing to take the Chanel or Armani off a woman's back." He'd learned in the weeks since arriving back here that those were her two favorite designers.

Pamela's only yield to self-consciousness was to tug the slipping scarf back over her ear before demanding, "What is the meaning of this?"

"Which this?" Mead asked, although he knew perfectly well what she was referring to.

"That *truck* in my driveway."

She pointed at it using her cell phone antenna, and Mead wondered if there might yet be a seventh message.

"Please tell me it's leased, or better yet, borrowed? But more important, what you were thinking to be driving without a license?"

"I have one. I renewed it first thing yesterday. After that I went to the dealership in town and bought this." He glanced back at the silver truck, then at Philo, who by that time—under the pretense of minding his own business—had retrieved two bags from the Cadillac's trunk. It was obvious by their color and make that the red-and black one on wheels was his mother's and the leather, travel-worn garment bag belonged to him. Wryly speculating as to whether the two bags had spent the night in the same hotel room, Mead called, "What do you think, Philo?"

The nearly bald-headed butler paused. There was no telling what was going on behind his sunglasses, but clearly he took his time to consider Pamela, Mead and then the truck.

"Competent 350 VA engine. Still, it's not a Corvette, is it?"

The fact that Philo knew he had driven the sports car in the old days when Mead hadn't known it—until Devan happened to mention it as she looked more closely at the truck this morning—had Mead narrowing his eyes. Was that a slam or a signal of sorts? And what had happened to the Corvette? Because it sure as hell wasn't in the four-car garage.

"You know your vehicles," was all he replied.

"My responsibilities lend themselves to a great deal of waiting. Reading and surfing the Internet is a useful time filler."

"Riveting, Philo," Pamela snapped. "Now would you mind bringing my bag inside while I finish this *private* conversation with my son?"

Since she barely wasted a glance at him, she missed seeing the way the corner's of Philo's thin mouth turned downward, but Mead caught the subtle reaction. *Careful, old girl, or you'll be calling an employment agency...or needing to hire a food taster.*

Without a word, Philo carried the luggage toward the house. Oblivious, Pamela wasted no time getting to the point.

"That thing is going back to the dealership. I am not paying to have this estate look like a common redneck's shack. It's bad enough the service people refuse to learn there's an auxiliary parking area for them behind the garage."

"First of all," Mead replied, "I don't know that a redneck, common or otherwise, could write a check for the amount this truck cost. Second, it's not your money, it's mine."

"Need I remind you, that while you have been incapacitated, I have been guardian of your estate?"

"I appreciate the TLC, but that's no longer necessary or desired." Mead made a mental note to ask Devan to recommend a good attorney, who could make that change legal and permanent.

About to speak, Pamela turned at the sound of another arrival. It was the Dreamscapes Lawn Care van and trailer. The driver parked only yards inside the gate, as Mead had noticed before, and two young men hopped out and began unloading the mowers. Which was Enrique and which was Pasquale, Mead didn't know, but he recalled their names from his conversation with Lavender.

Pamela extended her free hand, palm up as though offering evidence to a jury. "I rest my case. Well, let me tell you, I have about had it with those people. Can we possibly continue this conversation inside or must the rest of the help hear our personal business, too?"

It had been Mead's intent to change and head to Dreamscapes himself, but his mother's comment worried him. Reluctantly, he followed her up the sidewalk and, once inside, to her office. He paused in the middle of the room while she tossed her shoulder bag and phone onto the leather chair behind the ornate desk. Sliding off her sunglasses, she dropped them onto the leather blotter, next to a small stack of mail. Mead noticed that while she did indeed have on some cosmetics, it was the bare minimum and in fact accented her pale countenance and the deeper lines around her eyes and mouth.

Accepting that he might have been wrong about her

health, he asked, "Are the new blood pressure pills not agreeing with you?"

"I haven't started them yet. I want to finish those that I have first," she murmured absently as she quickly flicked through the mail.

No fan of being a pharmaceutical company's guinea pig, nevertheless, Mead could tell his mother's physical state was no more reassuring than her emotional one. "If the doctor thought that was a good idea, he wouldn't have upped your dosage in the first place."

"As if you care."

Mead didn't want her to think he'd forgotten her behavior the other evening, but if they were to continue living under the same roof—at least for the time being—they needed to try to get along. "I don't want to argue with you again. It's evident that you're not feeling well and—"

"Of course I'm not well! You ignore my calls. I ring here throughout the night and learn from a servant that you've been gone all night…what was I to think? You could be lying dead somewhere from foul play or otherwise. So after virtually a sleepless night, I cancel my other plans and race home to find you squandering your money and reverting to your old tomcat ways."

Inhaling a deep breath, Mead replied with studious patience. "I'm thirty-five. Unless something comes up, I don't have another medical checkup for six months, and if something happened to me, the police would have come to the house and informed whoever was here. As for the calls to my cell phone, I just didn't check."

"Why not? What good is the thing if you don't use it?"

"Next question."

"Oh. I see now. You were so busy that you forgot you had it."

"I was with a friend."

Crossing her arms, Pamela rounded the desk and strolled toward him. "A friend," she purred. "One of those friends who hasn't seen fit to come visit you all this time while you've been recuperating? One of those friends who never came to offer his sympathy and support to *me* when I first learned you were at death's door?" She paused at a high-backed chair and gripped its gilded trim. "You spent the night with Devan Anderson, didn't you? No, don't deny it," she continued when he opened his mouth to reply. "For once I can read your eyes. My God, the woman has cast some spell over you."

Under different circumstances, Mead might have cheerfully agreed.

"You lied to me," Pamela snapped bitterly. "You said you weren't having an affair."

"I did not lie. Then."

"What kind of a woman brings a man she's only known a week into her home, the bed that she'd shared with another man—with who knows how many men?"

"Be very careful," Mead warned. "You're about to step over a line that will force me to make a decision you don't want me to make."

"Good Lord, this is going from bad to worse. How could you? And her with a small child in the house."

Mead cared more about protecting Devan's reputation than escaping his mother's vitriol. "She would never do that. Devan has been working grueling hours. The Andersons have been keeping Blakeley on nights she's working late."

"Please don't insult my intelligence. She's working such grueling hours, yet she has the energy to seduce you?" Pamela's bosom heaved and her nostrils flared with her outrage. "No, I understand. She's figured out she's way in over her head ability-wise and financially with that business of hers and she's looking for a way out, a cushy life where her nails are properly manicured and she wouldn't be caught dead in a ponytail."

"Devan enjoys her work and the outdoors too much to be interested in nail polish and I think she looks great however she wears her hair." He might have said "sexy as hell" but his mother's anger was explosive enough without the admission.

Pamela shook her head and her voice dripped with revulsion and censure. "I couldn't be more disappointed in you. You think I don't understand that boys will be boys? It's that female."

The angrier Mead grew, the more quietly yet precisely he spoke. "Devan's an exceptional woman and a mother with strong principles."

"At least tell me you used birth control? Or have your southern regions allowed you to overlook that she's not below trapping you into marriage by getting pregnant?"

Something turned diamond-hard in Mead. "That's it."

As he headed for the door, Pamela struck her fist against the chair's wood trim. "Damn her—I wish she was dead!"

Now that the sun had reappeared, Devan had Jorges and the boys out at the estates working on the arbor. She remained back at Dreamscapes to finish a bid to do the landscaping for a new medical center off the interstate when her cell phone played the opening bar to Mozart's Fifth. Riley Walsh, she thought, with a silent groan.

"Devan, we have a problem," he began.

There was no sign of his usual glass-all-the-way-full cheeriness, and Devan knew why. "You've got that right. The check you said was on its way hasn't arrived."

Up front, Lavender looked up from instructing Nina Luna on arranging a candle display. Obviously, she'd heard that and knew who was on the line. She pantomimed gripping Riley by the throat and squeezing hard.

Giving her the thumbs-up sign, Devan waited for Riley's latest excuse.

"Never mind that. The storm wiped out half of the Stevensons' yard."

*Never mind?* Devan was so dumbstruck, she missed the name, not that it made any difference. "I'm not privy to your clients' names. Give me a location."

"Two thirty-seven Hillside Trail. The palms."

"Ah," she replied, picturing it immediately. "The palms that I warned you probably wouldn't survive our winter…the steep terracing and the lack of vegetation to keep it intact. I told you that you would have an avalanche if we got a heavy monsoon-type rain, but you didn't want to spend the extra money to do the job properly."

"Saying 'I told you so' isn't going to fix the problem. I need it taken care of today."

The nerve of the man, she fumed. Devan braced her elbow on the counter and her forehead in her hand. She would give a lot to still be at home with Mead. Dear heaven, would she ever.

To Riley, she replied, "Bring me a deposit and the check you owe us, and we'll discuss it." After she phoned the bank to inquire if both would clear.

"No can do. I had to go out of town again."

"Well, you'd better hustle back here because nothing is happening until you do. As a matter of fact, I'd be a fool not to pull my crew off the current site."

"I wouldn't try it if I were you."

So the amicable, good-old-boy mask was off. Devan's insides clenched at the barely veiled threat. "You're a piece of work," she told him. "You're lucky that you're dealing with us because at this stage, any other contractor would stand outside a Walsh house and warn potential buyers exactly what kind of sleaze you are."

"You can call me anything you want, darlin'. The fact remains I have you over a barrel and you don't have the reputation or business yet to survive without me. Now get that freaking yard fixed, or you'll speak to *my* attorney."

As soon as Devan disconnected, Lavender came over and laid a concerned hand on her back. "What's wrong?"

"I took that first contract with him, that's what's wrong." Sitting up, she eyed the petite teen meticulously following Lavender's orders and motioned her friend and partner to the back. Nina didn't need an earful of what she was about to say, and heaven knew she didn't want her worrying Jorges. "I swear I half hope the IRS or somebody makes his life as miserable as he's making ours."

Briefly, she relayed the problem. "And what irks me the most is the rat got off the phone before I could get a clue as to when he'll make good the invisible check."

Lavender gnawed at her frosted fuchsia lipstick. "What do you think we should do?"

Her worried expression brought out Devan's protective instincts and she immediately put her own concerns aside. "There's nothing we can do but make the repairs, bill Riley, and if he doesn't reimburse us, take him to court. I know we have the paperwork to eventually prove our claim. The problem is, he does have us in a no-win situation. We've got all that material for the other houses to pay for. We can't afford to take a time out while he gets a judge to hold us up risking our good credit with our suppliers. We just have to hope that he comes through with the funds as he always does."

"Well, I'm behind you a hundred percent," Lavender

told her. "If you think that's what we should do, then so be it, only how are you going to manage, hon?"

"Manage what?"

To Devan's delight and relief, Mead had arrived. They'd been so deep in conversation that neither of them had heard the bell sound up front. She'd known he would be coming to help as soon as he could change; however, he had taken somewhat longer than she'd expected. Considering everything else going on, her confidence had almost begun to waver. Seeing him now brought back all of the emotions she'd experienced a few hours ago, and she wanted nothing more than to run into his arms and beg him to take her someplace where they could relive their magical night all over again. As their gazes met, she saw that he was thinking much the same thing. There was something else there, too, that had her asking, "Are you okay?"

"Perfect now. So what's the problem."

"Riley strikes again," she said, and explained their latest crisis to him.

"What a—count me in."

Mead looked ready to inflict serious physical injury and Lavender giggled like a schoolgirl. "As cavalries go, you're hired, Mead." Lavender leaned closer to Devan. "Last time he was in here he said I didn't have to call him Mr. Regan. Can't say that for the rest of the family, can we?"

Devan nudged her with her elbow before giving him a soft, "Thanks."

"And he expects your vote to be mayor of this town?" Looking thoroughly disgusted, he placed his hands on his hips. "Tell me where I'll be of the most help?"

She yearned to step closer, reach inside his denim jacket and lean on that broad shoulder where she'd slept. Maybe he was tired, which was understandable considering he hadn't had any more sleep than she had, but he was resilient and stronger than ever. She wanted to believe he looked the best she'd seen him since his return. Common sense had her resisting taking him up on his offer.

"Are you sure? Isn't your mother due back from Dallas today?"

"She pulled in right behind me."

Devan glanced at her watch. "She must have left Dallas before dawn."

Glancing from one of them to the other, suddenly Lavender broke into a wide grin. "This is fascinating. Do go on."

"Lavender." Devan gave her a pleading look.

Showing no signs of being intimidated, Lavender winked at Mead. "I approve!"

"Before you go out into the street and make a public announcement," Devan warned, "remember we need both of our top accounts to survive."

"Aw, if Mead's mommy drops us, I won't sign 'Love Lavender' on her last invoice."

Seeing Mead's strange expression, Devan explained, "It's something she has in common with Goldie Hawn, who used to sign her school tests that way. This one even adds a 'Love, Lavender' on her IRS return."

Mead smiled politely. "Does it work?"

"Nah." Lavender wrinkled her nose. "They always send it back with a sticky note saying, 'Signature must match filer's full name.' Those folks could use a healthy dose of my mother's herbal laxative."

As Devan groaned, Mead touched her arm and said, "I'll pull my truck in back to your loading door."

The second he exited, Lavender collapsed limply on top of the worktable. "Wipe the drool from my chin, please."

"Isn't that the truth?" Devan replied. But as she went to open the overhead door, a small nagging something about Mead's demeanor had her worrying.

## Chapter Fifteen

When Devan lifted the overhead door, Mead sat waiting on the lowered tailgate of his Chevy. Parked beside the florist delivery van, it gave them a fair amount of privacy. Add that there was no one in the nursery yet, and that Devan's tender smile barely camouflaged worry and doubt, Mead gave in to the need driving him since leaving the house. He pulled her into the juncture of his thighs and kissed her with the urgency, desire and desperation of man who'd been shown a dream and then told it was forbidden to him. She came to him with the same honesty and passion that she'd given him last night and this morning, compounding the ache of inevitable loss growing inside him like the most cunning disease. His arms tightened, his kiss grew fierce because only she could heal him. But only he could destroy her.

Truth and the involuntary whimper telling him that he was in danger of physically marking her had him abruptly thrusting her to arm's length. Shaken to his core, he paced the width of the loading area to regain his composure.

"Flattering," Devan said, quietly once he faced her. "And terrifying. I knew something was wrong from the moment you came in and looked at me. What is it?"

All the way here he had struggled to find the words, the gentlest way to tell her without sending her world into a tailspin. Looking into the blue purity of her eyes, he realized Devan had a courage that surpassed his own. Her only requirement was total honesty.

"She knows."

"You *told* her we'd been together?"

"She knew. Look at me," he said, when she remained silent. "Isn't it as clear as your eyes? Lavender saw it."

But Devan was looking at something else. "This isn't just about her being furious and us losing her business. She scared you."

He sighed. "The only way she could."

"Now you're scaring me."

"I know. I wish there was a way to avoid that, but she said it, and while I have to believe it was a moment of blind jealousy and frustration, I'm not taking any chances with your safety."

"What?" Her eyes widening, Devan rasped, "She threatened me?"

"She said she wished you were dead."

Mead watched as she took in the ugly words and, as he feared, saw them draw blood.

"My God."

Aching to take her into his arms, he knew it was the last thing she wanted right now. She'd given him everything and he was bringing her world crashing down around her.

But as he watched her grow disturbingly pale, he couldn't remain silent.

"I'm here. You have enough going on. Let me worry about it and deal with her. She's already regretting the outburst. I doubt she's stupid or crazy enough to actually pull something."

"But you aren't sure."

Her quiet statement had him closing his eyes. With all his heart, Mead wished he could deny that, and his silence exposed his uncertainty.

With a heartrending cry, she launched herself at him. Mead barely caught her wrist in time to keep her from hurting herself, spun her around and spooned her against him, holding her tight.

"I'm here," he said again against her ear. "And I'll be here. Do you think I'd let anyone hurt you?"

"It's not me that I'm worried about, it's my child! Mead, what have you done?" she cried.

Steeling himself with grim acceptance, he told her. "Survived. I failed to come home in a casket. I realize that now. If I can't be the son—son, hell—the tool she wants, she would have preferred the other."

The psychological blow bent her at the waist and her anguish shook Mead to his core. "I'm sorry. I'm so damned sorry. If I could have kept this from you, I would, but I can't take the risk."

After several shaky gasps, she stilled, gripped his wrists to signal him to let her go. For a moment Mead thought he'd rather take another bullet, but as he forced himself to drop his hands, she turned to wrap her arms around him.

"Oh, Mead."

Almost weak with relief, he reclaimed what he thought

he'd lost. He held her to his heart and kissed every inch of her face before burying his against her neck.

"I've left the house," he said when he trusted his voice. "My things are in the truck and I'll get a room at the bed-and-breakfast off the square. But otherwise, I'm now your shadow."

Devan eased out of his arms to rub at her face and collect herself. "You know that's impractical as well as impossible. Besides, I'd want you to watch over Blakeley. No, we need to go to the police."

"And say what? The most powerful woman in the county, maybe the state, made a threatening remark? What's more, I'm the only person who heard it, and she's made it clear that she's willing to have me locked away if I try to expose her."

"How could she do that?"

Mead shrugged. "Lie. Use every resource at her disposal to get me out of the way. Hell, if I thought it would protect you, I'd leave town."

"No!"

He smiled and touched her cheek. "Thank you for that. You've just given me my life back a second time." But his pleasure was fleeting. "Pamela's vulnerable, Devan. That makes her dangerous. Everything changes from this moment forward."

Devan winced. "You can't even bring yourself to call her Mother."

"I despise her. I suspect I never had much respect for her— what you've told me about my life before seems to indicate that—but whatever there was she's managed to destroy."

Sighing, Devan rubbed at her temple. "I have to tell Lavender, Mead, and there's no way she can't tell Rhys, but that may be a good thing. This is his area of expertise.

Maybe he can offer some advice. But, oh, Lord, what do I do about Connie and Jerrold?"

"They'd never let Blakeley out of their sight, would they?"

"Not only that. Considering their increasing displeasure over me having a career, this news could have them seeking legal guardianship of Blakeley."

"Then let's hold off and see what Lavender's motorcycle man says."

Putting his arm around her, Mead led her back to the front of the building.

It was another hour before they made it to the damaged site. Lavender had been shaken at first, then angry as a swatted hornet for Devan, which earned additional points from Mead. She immediately paged Rhys, who was able to take a break and come over. He listened solemnly and asked a number of questions. In the end, though, he'd agreed there was little to be done unless Pamela actually tried something.

"You can't even get a restraining order," Rhys said, "until we've been called in to document some threat, verbal or otherwise."

But he had thanked them for confiding in him and assured them he would be keeping an eye out for any trouble. He'd also said he would need to have a confidential discussion with the chief. Mead hadn't been overly thrilled with that idea; however, Lavender's love interest soon set his mind at ease.

"Don't be fooled by how amiable he is to her in public. I've heard him come in from some function they've both been at and he's used the term 'Dragon Lady' several times."

Surreal as it was, an hour later Mead and Devan were back to her schedule standing at the scene of the flood catastrophe and gauging the damage. Life, Mead thought, did, indeed, go on, readily leaving you behind if you kept your pockets full of rocks.

Rocks and timber were the theme of the job in front of them. "How are you planning to get that muck back up the hill to make room to haul that landscaping material, too?" he asked Devan. It reminded him of some TV news report about California landslides he'd seen while recuperating.

Devan stared at the nightmare and the expression on her face told Mead she was remembering her warning to Riley.

"The old-fashioned way, I guess."

"I don't understand why someone who looks like you isn't selling BMWs instead of this. Look, your people love and respect you, sweetheart. But there's no way five shovels will fix this."

"You don't think I know that? Problem is, we can't afford to rent what we need. As it is, we're kissing every bit of profit goodbye."

Mead knew the day was taking a heavy toll on her without his part in it. He yearned to take her away, take her someplace where they could try to forget everything for a few hours. With that out of the question, he sought a resolution to the problem.

"I knew I'd had them put a trailer hitch on the back of my truck for a reason. Let's go to that rental place out by the car dealership and see what we can get. I'll pay for it," he said as she began to protest.

"I can't let you do that."

"You don't have a choice," Mead replied "I'm not going to let you kill yourself while you wait for Jorges and crew to finish up where they are and get over here. And if I were them, I'd take one look at this and run."

Common sense overrode Devan's battle between pride and principle. "I don't even know how to operate one of those things. Do you?"

"How hard can it be?"

It was more difficult than Mead imagined, but several hours later the disaster was removed and the timber was replaced with the proper drainage pipes finally included. Using the rented tractor, Mead then shoveled the dirt back into each tier. Darkness was upon them when they were finally ready to get to the replanting. Confident that Jorges would watch out for Devan, he returned the tractor and caught the owner as he was locking up and heading home.

He rejoined Devan and company and they worked by the grace of the new streetlights recently installed. It was almost nine when their little caravan returned to Dreamscapes.

A weary Jorges and dragging crew called or waved good-night and they drove off in his pickup. Devan locked up the van and returned the keys inside.

"I'll follow you to pick up Blakeley," Mead told her when she returned. Already aware of the Andersons' attitude over Devan's late hours, Lavender had encouraged Devan to let Blakeley go home with her. Mead approved, liking that the child would be under the care of a police officer, too.

She checked her watch, something that he'd noticed she did several times as the day waned.

"Too late. Lavender has already put her to bed. I don't like to disrupt her rest or shuttle her around in the night air once she's asleep."

She looked so guilt-ridden, Mead put his arm around her and had to urge her to her vehicle. "I'm sorry, sweetheart. I know holding your little girl would be the best medicine right now. Come on. I'll follow you home and see you're locked up tight."

It wasn't what he wanted, but as he drove behind Devan, he knew she had to be as physically wiped out as she'd been yesterday, and mentally considering a Vacancy sign. He'd tear off a strip of his skin before imposing on her, but the truth was, he could probably jog to Dallas and back, and if she'd open her arms to him, he would make love to her until they both passed out from exhaustion.

When he pulled in beside her SUV, he killed the engine and climbed out to wait for her to get her mail. She didn't need to know he scanned each end of the street for something suspicious. Following her to the door, he waited as she unlocked it and turned off the alarm.

"Will you go pick up Blakeley to get her changed before work in the morning?" he asked once she got that part done.

"Yes, about seven-thirty."

Inwardly, he high-fived himself that he was beginning to read her and not just guess. "I'll be here at seven-twenty—"

The phone cut him off.

"I'll bet that's Lavender," Devan said. "I promised to call when I got home and I'll bet she thinks I've forgotten. Maybe Rhys has something more to say."

She hurried to the kitchen and Mead stepped inside, shutting the door so as not to let any more heat escape than necessary. He expected to hear her trying to get a word in edgewise, but instead she hung up and returned to him.

One glance at her troubled expression and he asked, "What?"

"I'm not sure. No one spoke. I've been meaning to sign up for caller ID ever since we began the business, but I just haven't gotten around to it."

"Do you get those kinds of calls?"

"Not in ages. Years."

Mead didn't like the sound of that at all. "That cinches it, then. I'm camping out on your couch. Go call Lavender, and I'll go get my things and lock up my truck."

To his surprise and relief, she didn't try to argue with him, but he hated seeing worry leaden her shoulders and take the light from her face. As for the call, who knew? It could be a coincidence. Damned if he would take any chances, though.

Once he returned, he could hear her talking and from the context knew she was speaking with her friend. Locking the front door and setting the alarm, he went to the kitchen doorway and mouthed, "Shower." Then he went to the master bathroom and stripped.

He had his hands braced on the wall and his head under the steaming hot spray when he heard the door open and Devan stepped inside.

"Need someone to wash your back?"

He sent up a brief prayer of thanks for whatever it was that made her forgive him for turning her world inside out. "I'd better warn you," he said, "if you start anything, there's no way I can sleep on the couch."

She poured some citrus-scented soap into her hand and lathered it up. Then she began working it over his shoulders and back. "You're the one who brought up the couch."

Mead didn't know what he responded to more, the unmistakable meaning behind her words or her hands on his body. He closed his eyes as she worked the lather over his skin, her touch alternately soothing as she massaged and firm as she kneaded stiffer muscles. "This is so hard on you."

"Being with you…touching you again," she murmured. "It's hard time I deserve."

Between the hot spray and sensuous massage, he wasn't

sure he heard her correctly. Then she was touching her lips
to a knife scar under his left shoulder blade. Guessing what
she was thinking, he sought to ease her worry.

"My records say that was from combat training."

"What did they use, rusty can openers?"

Hearing her voice break, Mead turned. She fought and
won her battle with tears, but just barely.

"Devan…my heart."

Intent on kissing her, Mead was stunned to see her cover
her face with her hands.

"I'm sorry."

Mead dropped his hands…started to reach for her again,
then yanked the shower door open and got out. Blinded by
the vision of her covering her face, he grabbed a towel.
He'd believed she saw him beyond scars both outside and
in. He'd hoped his vow to protect her from Pamela, his
steadfast loyalty today, would offset at least some of the
injustice heaped on her.

Wrapping the towel around his waist, he sought his
clothes, but his bag wasn't where he'd left it. Exiting to the
bedroom, he found it on the chaise.

"Mead!"

Devan rushed to him and stayed the hand about to yank
on the bag's zipper. "What did I do?"

"Nothing. You're perfect. But *my* dream… I was a fool to
imagine I could be yours. You warned me. I saw what I
wanted to see, but I come with too much baggage, an uncertain future—" He spun around and drank in her beauty one
last time. Devan stood in front of him a glistening goddess
in the glow of the bathroom light. "I want you so much I'd
accept your sweet compassion. Hell, I'd try to buy you—it
*is* a family tradition we're good at. Problem is I don't know
if I can live with waiting for you to leave me for the real thing."

New tears filled Devan's eyes. "The real thing? You can't tell? You haven't listened? Being with you then, finally being with you again, ruined me for anyone else ever. It's a guilt I live with."

Mead couldn't keep from touching her. He cupped her face with his right hand. "But you want who I was. Whenever you touch my scars, you freeze up."

"Anyone who loves you would! And for the record, you had one or two back then, too. Each is a symbol of pain you endured, your courage, and a reminder that I shouldn't be this blessed. Do you think I want to feel this much? Why do you think I struck out at you today? What I feel terrifies me. What people I love risk because of that—"

"Love. My love."

Mead reached for her and the arms that crushed her to him might as well have been steel. Mine, he thought tilting his head back as she pressed her lips to where his heart slammed hardest with emotion, and not just my dream... my life.

Devan reached up to draw his head down, sought his mouth. When he locked his to hers, he lifted her high in his arms then let her slide slowly down the length of him until they both shuddered with the hunger it released in them. Their kiss grew from searching to demanding and possessive.

Lifting her again, Mead stepped to the bed and, blindly reaching for the turned-down covers, swept them farther back. Then he placed one knee on the bed and slowly, slowly lowered them both across it, until he crushed her into it. But she gloried in his weight, her arms strong as she held him tighter.

Fatigue forgotten, tomorrow's fears, too, he moved

against her, drinking the low moan as she felt his hardness and hunger. His own moan was sheer masculine pleasure as she slid her hands down to his hips and her fingers bit into muscle to urge him closer.

Wanting her hunger, wanting her to take anything she would from him, he rolled them over in a tangle of limbs until she lay over him. She bathed him with her heat and her kisses, licked the moisture in the shallow hollow at the base of his throat like a kitten lapping milk, nipping at a taut bicep, teasing his already hard nipple with her warm breath, her tongue and finally her teeth. Whenever she came to an old wound, she paused to first look at him before offering a healing kiss.

Mead couldn't take his eyes off her, half-afraid she would vanish. She moved with the same grace he admired by day, but which became more liquid whenever she touched him. That ignited yet a greater fire in him, so that he had to touch her, too, but she never remained still long enough for him to give her the pleasure she was bringing him. And yet when she sat up and straddled him, her gifted hand inviting him into her, he discovered she was as ready for him as he was for her.

Uttering a hoarse sound as she sheathed him, Mead rolled them again, needing to be deeper, wanting to get closer, to touch as much of her as possible. Then slowly moving inside her, he heard a thin sigh as his name. He did it again, patient, so they both could feel every sensation of their union.

With an involuntary shake of her head, she tightened around him in an effort to keep him still.

"Look at me," he rasped. When she did, he thrust harder into her tightness and saw passion shimmer in every blue shard of her crystalline eyes.

"Again," she entreated, her voice low.

"I love you," he said as he gave himself to her.

With an almost keening cry, Devan drew his head down and sought his mouth, wrapped her legs around his waist. Gripping her hips, Mead drove them both to bliss.

Minutes later, when they were settled against the pillows and warmed by the covers against the night's descending chill, Mead held Devan and listened to her slip deeper into sleep. Seeing how even then her lips sought his skin for an unconscious kiss, his heart swelled to near bursting and he gently lifted the hand resting in the mat of chest hair to his mouth.

Although set low, the ringing of the phone had him snatching it to keep Devan from waking. She stirred slightly, but then snuggled closer to him before drifting back into her peaceful slumber.

Mead lifted the receiver to his ear and waited. Waited.

The silence on the other end lengthened.

Mead could almost hear the question coming through the line. Then abruptly the caller slammed down the phone.

Replacing his receiver, he wrapped his arm protectively around Devan and stared up at the ceiling, his face a stony mask, his eyes dark with a warrior's determination

## *Chapter Sixteen*

The next morning Chief of Police Bart Marrow telephoned Dreamscapes just as Devan and Lavender were doing their daily synchronizing of orders and plans. Mead was already out back helping with the loading. Devan hadn't had much contact with the forty-something-year-old career peace officer, but when she had, she'd found him to be no-nonsense, yet pleasant. Still, her heart skipped a beat when he introduced himself.

"Yes, Chief," she said. Meeting Lavender's wide-eyed look, she shrugged.

"Mrs. Anderson, would you and Mr. Regan mind coming down to my office? As you probably know, Officer Atwood has told me something that's disturbing and I'd like to discuss it with you."

"Of course. You just caught us as we were leaving for a job site, but we could come there first."

"I'll be waiting for you."

Hanging up, Devan asked Lavender, "Did Rhys say anything else about Chief Marrow's reaction to our story?"

"Just what I told you last night, that the chief asked why you hadn't come down to file a report documenting the event. Rhys took responsibility for that, telling him that since they couldn't act upon a complaint until called to the scene, it was relatively useless. The chief is a stickler for details, though, and he said that in the future, he wanted a charge of that magnitude documented anyway and told Rhys to write it up and start a file. Then he thanked Rhys for keeping him informed."

"Well, he wants to see us right now."

"So I heard. You'd better go then. I see Nina coming back from saying good morning to that cute little Eduardo," she said, referring to their most recent employee who kept things watered in the nursery and toted plants to customers' vehicles. "We'll be fine. Just let me know the skinny afterward."

"That reminds me—" Devan frowned "—have you been having any hang-up calls?"

"Nah. Not since I went to that condom store to buy that gorgeous hunk something fun for Valentine's Day and that creepy guy checked me out. I should have paid in cash instead of writing a check with all of my personal information on it. But he said he didn't have change for a fifty. In a busy place like that? Alarms should have gone off in my head."

"I remember now," Devan replied. "Rhys followed your hunch and paid him a visit."

"And the guy quit and vamoosed shortly afterward." Lavender sighed. "My hero."

"Sounds like a keeper to me."

Devan went to get Mead but paused to compliment Nina on her new butter-yellow camisole and peasant skirt. The girl was blossoming with her first job, and no matter how colorful or eccentric Lavender looked, she was proving an inspiring teacher and mentor.

But once Devan continued into the nursery, her smile grew into a troubled frown. What if Chief Marrow knew of something that had occurred overnight? Seeing Mead had spotted her and was coming to meet her lifted her spirits somewhat. Considerably, she amended, seeing the intimate message in his eyes.

Although he remained conscious and respectful of her position as employer to the men behind him and barely caressed her shoulder when they met, his look and tone vibrated with possessiveness and concern. "Something's up?"

"Chief Marrow has asked us to stop by before we head out to Manor Estates. It's about his conversation with Rhys yesterday…I think."

"But you feel it's more?"

"He could have stopped by and casually mentioned that he was aware of things and would stay on top of them, I don't know. This feels like a summons, exactly what you said you'd worried about."

Mead glanced over her head a moment, then asked, "Should the subject come up, how much do you want to expose about us?"

"Everything."

In that instant Mead looked as though he was about to gobble her up like the last dessert in Texas. "Maybe not everything," he replied thickly. "After all, there are parts you still need to reintroduce me to."

"Deal," Devan whispered.

"Go tell your people what you need to, and I'll be ready when you are."

The chief had apparently given word that they would be coming. The moment they entered, a woman Devan recognized from somewhere but didn't know stood from the dispatcher's desk and led them the few yards to the corner office.

Chief Bart Marrow was an attractive, calm-natured man, who looked like he would enjoy golf or chess over sweaty group sports or gym machine drills. His salt-and-pepper hair matched the shading of his neat mustache and his pale gray eyes.

Stepping around his desk, he shook hands and invited them to sit. "I know your time is precious," he said, "but can we offer you coffee?"

Devan and Mead both declined.

Marrow returned to his seat and studied the thin folder lying open on his desk. "I appreciate this is a sensitive matter and I want you to know it's in our best interest as much as yours to keep things under wraps and forgotten if this turns into nothing. But, Mr. Regan, you should know that your mother phoned me personally around midnight last night. She wanted it to be a 911 but without the public-accessible records."

"That sounds like her MO"

Marrow nodded, his expression remaining impartial. "On occasion, she's been known to suggest she knows better than we do how to conduct our business. However, when she or anyone states a concern regarding a relation meeting with foul play, it needs to be considered with respect."

"She knew where I was, Chief. Her problem was that I'd moved out of the house."

Bart Marrow's straight, thin lips twitched. "You are of the age of consent. Problem is—as you're undoubtedly aware—you've been in her guardianship due to your combat injuries."

"The doctors have released me. So far the bank has cashed my checks. The state renewed my license."

Leaning back in his chair and crossing an ankle over a

knee, the chief replied, "Sounds good to me. On the other hand, tell me what I'm looking at if TV satellite trucks, choppers bearing celebrity reporters and Elvis come racing to Mount Vance as the next story du jour?"

"I could say you should leave that to Mrs. Regan, Chief," Mead began. "In her usual gracious fashion, she would likely make an allowance for network choppers to land on the estate's level lawns, and satellite trucks could park on the mile-and-a-quarter paved driveway—not because of whatever brings them to town, sir, but because she'll be convinced they're really there to interview her." Steepling his fingers, he added, "Elvis… would be iffy. And common folk make her break out in hives. But that's why she built the Red Wall of Regan around the estate."

Marrow cleared his throat behind his fist. "Would Mrs. Anderson qualify as the latter in her estimation?"

Mead turned to look at Devan. "It would be her most erroneous and foolish assumption if she did."

Admiring Mead's ability to keep his cool, Devan was slow to notice that Chief Marrow switched his focus to her.

"Would you mind my asking how long you've known Mr. Regan, ma'am?"

"We were both born here," she replied with a shrug.

The chief stroked his mustache as though choosing his words carefully. "It's distasteful for me to pry into personal business and I apologize in advance for the slightest indication that I have, but after Mrs. Regan's phone call last night, I did drive by your residence and saw two vehicles parked there. Each, as you well know, is registered to one of you."

Devan saw Mead shift, knew he'd already heard enough and had endured his fill. "Chief Marrow," she said quietly, "we have nothing to hide. Is there something specific you need to know?"

"Thank you. Officer Atwood told me about your claim that Mrs. Regan threatened you, Mrs. Anderson."

"Mead told me she did," Devan replied.

"But you have no proof?"

"I know someone called my house last night and when I asked who was there, no one answered."

"And from that one incident—"

"It happened twice," Mead interjected. At Devan's confused glance, he told her, "You'd fallen asleep."

She could feel heat flood her cheeks and not just because he was trying to protect her.

"No caller ID?" the chief asked.

Devan sighed. "Only an answering machine, but I plan to rectify that error at the first opportunity."

Once again Chief Marrow studied them. "Are we dealing with a mother's jealousy, Mr. Regan?"

"I don't know, Chief. It must appear that way to someone on the outside looking in, and as you can imagine, I'm hampered by having no history to compare it with, but—" Mead struggled to find and speak the right words. "Since I've returned, I've never gotten the impression that she's emotionally connected to anyone. It's not a question of why did I move out, but why didn't I move out years ago? And more important than that, who was my father that he could bear to stay married to her?"

The heartbreaking statement didn't leave the seasoned cop unaffected; however, except for a sigh, he was too much the professional to expose more. "Those are questions worthy of asking a doctor, although I suspect you've had your fill of them for a while."

Mead grunted. "You can say that again."

"It has struck me—and I hope you won't take this the wrong way—that what's happened to you, as costly as it was in so many ways, ended up as a blessing."

Reaching over to cover Devan's clasped hands with his own, Mead said, "The thought has occurred to me."

"All right." Sitting up, Chief Marrow leaned forward to rest his forearms on his desk blotter. "Aside from my earlier question, I just needed to gauge whether I should worry about you losing your cool and taking matters into your own hands."

"The only way to reassure you is if you make damn certain nothing happens to Devan or her daughter."

Bart Marrow nodded grimly. "I'd feel the same way in your shoes, but you didn't hear me say that." He rose and held out his hand to Devan. "It appears to me that I need to have a little heart-to-heart with Mrs. Regan."

The rest of the day seemed anticlimactic to Devan, at least until the evening. They worked diligently at Manor Estates. Even so, it was closing in on eight when they pulled into Dreamscapes. Devan had mixed emotions— there was time to get Blakeley, after all, but that would mean she wouldn't spend the night in Mead's arms.

"Don't brood," Mead said, enfolding her close once Jorges and the young men drove away. "You said yourself that Blakeley cried when you told her she might have to sleep over at her grandparents' again, and as much as it pleases me to know you want me, I sense how much you need to hold your child, sweetheart."

He was right, of course. Blakeley was undoubtedly hearing things that upset and confused her. And Devan needed to show Jerrold and Connie that she was doing everything in her power not to use their goodwill. "Want to come over for breakfast in the morning? It would give Blakeley another chance to get used to having you around."

"Sounds like a plan. First things first, though…" Mead angled his head and took Devan's mouth for a long, tantalizing kiss. By the time he lifted his head, he was hard and cupping her bottom to lift her against him. "Me and my big mouth. You don't know what torture it is to have to watch this little tush," he muttered squeezing her, "and not be able to do anything about it."

"Uh-huh, and it's so fair of you to whisper sweet naughties in my ear when the others are within hearing distance or paying attention."

"You think I don't want you to miss me, too?"

"You know I will," she replied, rising on tiptoe for another kiss.

By the time Devan was in her SUV, she was feeling seriously achy and couldn't help squirming in her seat to find a comfortable position. At that moment, she happened to look over to see Mead grinning wickedly from his truck. "Stinker," she said.

He insisted on following her to the Andersons', but parked several houses away to make sure everything was all right.

Devan tugged her denim jacket closed as she ran up the sidewalk and rang the doorbell. At least the chill would be a good way to explain why her cheeks were flushed, she thought.

Devan expected her usual welcoming smile, but Connie looked self-conscious and barely made eye contact as she unlocked the storm door. "Devan. What are you doing here?"

A bit startled, Devan laughed. "The obvious."

"Well, of course, but—" Connie stepped back for her to enter "—Blakeley is in bed."

Devan checked her watch. "It's a half hour early. Is she feeling all right?"

"She's probably a bit blue. Her grampa insisted because she talked back to him at dinner."

"Oh, dear. I can't imagine why. She knows to respect her elders. What happened?"

Wrapping her arms around herself, Connie glanced into the living room as though afraid to be overheard. "She refused to eat the lima beans he put on her plate."

"Mom, you know she can't eat them." Devan wasn't pleased that one of the few instructions she'd given them had been ignored. "The skins are too heavy for her tummy to digest and she throws up." She herself had found that out the hard way.

"There were only a few. She just got stubborn and Jerrold—on point of principle—had to teach her a lesson and tell her she either cleaned her plate or she wouldn't get ice cream and she could go to bed without any dinner. She said that was fine with her and she wanted her mommy."

Devan couldn't believe what she was hearing. "You should have called me. That's not teaching her anything, that's abuse. She wasn't being stubborn or rude, she was protecting her body. I'm seriously disappointed in his behavior and you allowing him to do it."

"He's my husband, the head of our household."

"And wrong!" Her voice shook and she wanted to speak to her father-in-law before she got too emotional. "Where is he? You know this isn't the first time his actions have disturbed me. He's said things in front of my daughter that she shouldn't hear, and are offensive and unfair to me."

"He's not feeling well and went to bed early himself."

"As usual he leaves you to do his unpleasant work for him."

Tight-lipped, Connie replied, "That's uncalled for, Devan."

"You mean, I'm fair game, but you two are above criticism? It doesn't work that way. And before we go any further and say something we can't take back, I'm going to get my daughter and take her home."

"You don't have to take her out into the cold and risk her catching a cold just because we offered constructive criticism and advice," Connie said. "It increasingly looks to me that you need it."

Devan froze in midstep. She couldn't believe what she was hearing. "What became of the people I saw as my surrogate parents? I thought I knew you, that you loved and approved of me. I worked so hard to mold myself so you would."

"That goes without saying, dear. Jay had impeccable taste and you were his princess. That's how we'll always see you. So in this day and age when crime occurs next door, how can you want to drive the streets and take a child to an empty house where it's just the two of you?" Connie fidgeted with her wedding ring, something she'd done for as long as Devan had known her. "It is just the two of you, isn't it?"

Devan didn't know if she could take much more. She felt like someone shipwrecked on a pile of crumbling rocks and every few hours a wave disintegrated what remained of her world. "That's what this is about. If you have something to say, surely we've been close long enough for you to speak your mind frankly? Why this evasiveness?"

"Because I hate gossip and don't want to spread it."

"You believe it, though. If you didn't, you wouldn't be saying such things to me."

"All right, but please don't tell her that I was the one to betray her. I ran into Bev Greenbriar at the Garden Club."

Devan held up her hand. "Stop there. You've said all I need to know."

"Well, that's interesting," Connie said, gaining courage. "I hit a nerve, didn't I?"

"You got it right the first time—Beverly is one of the biggest mouths I've ever met and it's no pleasure to claim her as a Mount Vance native. I think she lives to stir up trouble, and do you know why? Because she recognized early on she has no other talents."

"Say what you will, it took her to tell me you had a stranger staying in Jay's home last night."

A rush of reactions flooded Devan's mind. Few of them were appropriate to repeat. One had to be made clear, though. "Connie, you know I want you to be a big part of Blakeley's life—and mine. But that house is mine, and not just because Jay is gone. He didn't buy it for me. We bought it together. I didn't come to my marriage empty-handed. And this is no longer an era when women can be brainwashed into believing they're subservient to their husbands."

Connie played with the ring again. "I have loved my life."

"It's all you've known. Except for three months as the cashier at the hospital gift shop, and your volunteering, you don't know what any of the rest of us are talking about, let alone coping with."

"At least I haven't desecrated my husband's reputation sleeping with a stalker and possible mental case."

To think she had considered this woman "Mom." Devan knew that was over. "Not that it's anyone's business, including yours, but no one has been at the house overnight if she's there. Now excuse me, I'll collect my daughter and leave you to your perfect, germ-free, suffocating world."

She hurried down the hall to the guest room where she found Blakeley mewing in her sleep as she huddled in the wicker chair, her coat on and her backpack in her lap. The image broke her heart.

Scooping the child and her possessions into her arms, Devan whispered, "Time to go, darlin'."

"Mommy!" Blakeley clutched at her with all the force of her four-year-old body, burying her face against her jacket as Devan carried her down the hall.

"Good night, Blakeley," Connie said primly as she waited at the door. "I'll see you tomorrow."

Feeling her daughter's arms tighten around her, Devan replied, "Tomorrow being Halloween, I think I'll keep her with me. She'd enjoy seeing all that's going on in and around town."

"Oh. Well, don't forget to bring her by for her treat. We'll enjoy seeing her costume."

Neither of them responded and Devan hurried down the sidewalk to her SUV. The sound of the Andersons' door closing and Connie setting the lock echoed something finalizing inside her.

"Devan?"

She gasped when a shadow separated itself from a tree along the road. "Mead, you almost gave me a heart attack."

"That goes both ways. Another few seconds," he told her, reaching to open the back door, "and I'd have to have gone inside to check on you."

"I'm sorry. Things…it's crazy. I'll tell you about it when I get her in her own bed."

"I'll be right behind you."

On the ride home Blakeley barely spoke, but when she did it was with a clarity that committed Devan to life-altering change.

"I don't want to go there no more, Mommy."

"I'm so sorry, darlin'. I wish I could have gotten to you sooner."

"I closed my eyes and told you and told you."

Devan swallowed against the painful lump in her throat. "We'll get you home and changed into your toastiest pj's and figure out what you want to eat."

At the house, Mead helped get Blakeley inside. "Give me a few minutes and I'll be right back," she told him. "Help yourself to anything you want."

"I'd feel better if there was something more I could do."

Devan knew what comfort her daughter would enjoy most, and it was simple enough, but not for someone with Mead's memory challenge. "There's milk in the fridge and chocolate syrup in the pantry. Do you think you can make a mug of hot chocolate? Well, not too hot. There's also cinnamon bread in the refrigerator. If you'll put a slice in the toaster—"

"I've got you covered."

"She likes a little butter on it."

"I think so would I."

Devan had Blakeley tucked in her bed and surrounded by her favorite stuffed animals when Mead knocked at the door bearing a tray. As soon as she saw it, Devan smiled.

The cocoa and toast were there all right, and so was a marshmallow snowman.

"Trick-or-treat," he said, wiggling "Marshman" at her child. He held up the figure to inspect it more closely and added, "Don't try eating the head or hat. I don't think peppercorn eyes and ink mouth tastes very good."

For the first time that evening Blakeley smiled.

"He's silly."

Mead winked at Devan and left mother and daughter to the snack.

Several minutes later Devan found him in the kitchen standing by the back door. The readiness in his stance made her think of how she had watched for him. Wondering exactly what he was thinking about in their unexpected journey, she put the tray on the counter and stepped into his extended arms.

"I don't know what I'm going to do," she told him. "If this was all we needed to deal with, I'd probably have reacted differently, but Mead, this changes things for me."

"What happened?"

She told him about Jerrold's behavior, Connie's lack of intervention...then the real reason behind their disappointing trend. "The woman with the obnoxious dog. They would rather believe Bev Greenbriar than respect me for trying to do nothing less than what their son did—fulfill dreams and take care of family."

"If I was out of the picture, they'd ease up on you."

"Or tighten the noose and sap me dry." Devan held him tighter. "Don't even think that as a bad joke. No, no more toeing a line I don't understand. No more standing there to be politely, verbally chiseled down to what's socially acceptable. As grateful as I am for their help in a crunch, I'd be a fool to continue. I won't watch my daughter become an unhappy clone."

Devan looked up at him. "Mead, I don't want you to go away tonight. I'm not asking you to sleep on the couch, I'm asking you to sleep in the guest room. Besides, it's the least I can do, since you're helping us so much and you won't let us pay you."

"I'd be happier if you're offering because you can't stand the idea of me being even a mile away from you."

"There's that, too."

He pressed his cheek to the top of her head. "You think Blakeley will be okay with that?"

"I do."

"Then it's a deal. I'd planned on camping out in your driveway anyway."

\* \* \*

Devan's decision to keep Blakeley with her all day was an impulsive one that could have been problematic, but, thanks to Lavender, Halloween went from a logistics challenge to one of whimsy and creativity for her daughter.

While Mead had showered, Devan had called her partner at home to warn her that life had grown degrees more complicated. Lavender didn't disappoint. First thing in the morning as Blakeley burst into the florist shop, she sang, "Aunt Lah-di-dah! I'm here!"

Lavender popped up from behind a display table of ceramic and candle jack-o'-lanterns, black cats and ghosts, complete with a smoking kettle in the center. Her face was painted an iridescent green that matched her green hair extensions. "Who be dat? Blakeley Buglet? *Yum!* Come hop into this pot of little girl stew," she said with a witch's cackle.

"I'm Wendy!" Blakeley ran to her, as much to show off how her ringlets bounced as her blue granny-style gown that she wore over a white turtleneck and jeans to stay warm. "Mommy said I can wear my costume all day, and that if I asked pretty, you'd find a blue ribbon for my hair to match my dress."

"I sure can," Lavender said, rising. "You're out to dazzle Peter Pan, huh? I know just the ribbon back here by my worktable. Tinkerbell will have an electric short she'll be so jealous at how gorgeous you'll look."

As Lavender slapped on a painter's cap, Devan eyed her matching white oversize coveralls and asked, "Who are you supposed to be?"

"Priscilla the Painter Witch, of course. Neon Nina and I will be manning the face-painting booth at the Festival on the Square tonight, remember? And we're hoping Blakeley—I mean, Wendy—will help us finish preparing our costumes."

Although she smiled, inwardly Devan sighed, sorry that her in-laws didn't appreciate what a good friend and partner she had in Lavender. While Devan spent the day at her landscaping work, Lavender would watch over her daughter. A born mother if she'd ever met one, Lavender was. Devan knew Blakeley couldn't be in better hands.

"Mead is bringing in the cot," she said. "Please don't let her talk you out of making her take a nap or the little minx will be too tired tonight."

"We'll be fine! Just don't think because tall, dark and handsome is around that you can get away with not wearing your costume."

"Peter Pan never looked better," Mead drawled as he strolled beside Devan at the festival.

She was glad it had warmed up again; otherwise her green suede vest over matching shorts and the green tights would have left her freezing. Giving the cap Lavender had made for her a jaunty tilt, Devan grinned at him. "You're just being a flatterer because you're relieved you don't have to dress up and be silly."

"Someone has to beat off the guys ogling your legs and that sweet tush."

"*Mead.*"

Earlier, they had taken Blakeley trick-or-treating up and down their street, carefully avoiding the Greenbriar house. On the way here, Devan had casually suggested to her daughter that they also do Nana and Grampa's street, but Blakeley grew pouty.

"I don't want to, Mommy."

It would probably cause repercussions later, but Devan didn't want to ruin her little girl's day.

"What's next?" Mead asked.

They had watched a puppet show, played a game or two, and Blakeley had gotten a star painted on her face at Lavender and Nina's booth. Blakeley told everyone who paused to watch or get in line to have their faces painted that she had made their costumes all by herself. The coveralls were splattered with bright paint and each backside had two little handprints on them.

Devan pointed with her orange carnation. Adorned with a black ribbon bearing the MVHS initials in gold, the flowers were another of Lavender's ideas, the proceeds pledged to the high school band for their fund-raising efforts to go to the Rose Bowl Parade. From the number of them she'd seen around the square, Dreamscapes would be able to deliver a handsome check. "Sugar Lane, and that should do it."

They passed the noisiest booth, run by the band. Lavender's Rhys was just climbing out of the heated pool, having been successfully dunked by one of the students.

"No fair," he complained, grinning. "The Mustang's star pitcher should be disqualified."

Rhys was dressed in a convict's orange coveralls. The current mayor was wearing a Santa costume and his soggy beard was beginning to sag, exposing his chin, while the band director was Elvis.

They were passing the gazebo where several band members who had started their own music group were playing. Suddenly, Mead's fingers tightened on Devan's arm. She looked up at him, only to see his face become a stony mask.

"What is it?" she asked. Following his gaze, she saw Pamela, along with several candidates, handing out political buttons at a voter's registration booth. She had spotted them, as well, and her fake smile grew even more brittle. "Let's just keep walking."

Fortunately the square was teeming with townspeople enjoying the mild weather and festivities, and no one appeared to notice that mother and son hadn't spoken.

"Thank goodness Riley isn't around," Devan said when they were past the booth. "I suspect he'd have had the audacity to try to strike up a conversation." Today yet another check had bounced and she'd left a message on his answering machine that she was pulling her crew off the Manor Estates projects. It seemed that even his secretary was tired of interceding with empty assurances. They still had a few jobs elsewhere to do and with the other holidays coming wouldn't feel the financial crunch for a while, but she would be worrying about what they already had invested in Walsh Development soon enough.

Trying not to let him or the presence of Pamela mar what had been a fun evening, Devan got Blakeley's ticket to Sugar Lane. "Here you go, sweetie," she said, giving it to her. "Go get in line."

Sugar Lane was a clever trail of giant PVC candy canes and foam lollipops. Lit by hundreds of feet of twinkling lights, it all framed barrels of candies donated by various businesses, organizations and private citizens. Children with tickets could take their bags or pumpkins and walk through collecting candy.

"We'll be waiting for you at the other end," she told Blakeley.

When she reached Mead, she asked for her digital camera, which he had tucked into the pocket of his leather jacket.

"Is she having fun?" he asked, handing it over.

"And how...but you're not." He hid it well; however, it was clear that he wasn't all that comfortable with being stared at, and when some people stopped them and politely reintroduced themselves, he'd been gracious, but add the Pamela sighting and Devan could tell he was ready to call it a day.

"I'm with you," he murmured, stepping behind her and taking hold of her shoulders. "That's all that matters." He peered over the heads of those blocking Devan's view. "Here she comes."

Devan excused herself and eased up front to take Blakeley's picture. She'd taken several others along the way. "Did you enjoy that?" she asked her.

"Yeah. Look how full my pumpkin is now! When we get home, I'm gonna spread it all on the table and pick out my favorites. Then you can give the rest to Lavender for the store's candy dish."

"How thoughtful. We should put a note on the jar," she said, winking at Mead. "Blakeley's Leftovers."

Giggling, Blakeley reached inside. "I'm so starved, I'm gonna have one now."

"Just one, and watch where you're walking or you'll stumble and we'll be picking up candy for an hour."

In the next instant the plastic pumpkin did drop to the ground and Blakeley screamed. *"Mommeeeee!"*

Devan watched in horror as Blakeley lifted her hand to her. There was an ugly slash across her small palm and blood began flooding out at an alarming speed.

## Chapter Seventeen

"Oh, my God—baby! Mead!"

Devan barely got that much out before Mead swept a wailing Blakeley into his arms and took swift command of the terrible scene.

"Grab that bucket," he told her grimly. "The piece on the ground by your boot—careful how you pick it up. *Anyone*," he shouted to the gaping and increasingly upset crowd. "Find me a clean white towel, napkin, anything!"

Someone rushed over with a whole handful of paper napkins from the dispenser at a nearby concession booth. "The ambulance is parked on the far side of the square," the man told them.

"I remember seeing it, thanks," Mead replied. "Sweetie—" he shifted Blakeley in his arms to show her what to do "—you have to clasp your hands and hold the napkins to the wound as tight as you can to stop the flow of blood. I've got you, you don't have to worry about slipping."

"It h-h-hurts," she wailed.

"I know. We'll get it fixed in no time." As soon as Devan rose with the candy-filled pumpkin, he told her, "Run!"

Amid calls of "Shut down Sugar Lane!" and "All candy back to the ticket booth!" by the event's organizers, and shouts for the police, Devan and Mead raced across the square as fast as they could get people to make way for them. From his higher vantage point Rhys spotted them and signaled to the uniformed officer nearest him, who soon made that easier for them.

As they passed an alarmed Lavender and Nina, Devan shouted, "The candy has been tampered with! I'll call!"

The officer had already notified the EMTs, who had the ambulance doors open and ready. Mead passed Blakeley to the man inside, then took the pumpkin and handed it to the cop. "It's the chocolate bar on top," he told him. Barely pausing to breathe, he lifted Devan up into the ambulance. "I'll get my truck and meet you there." Although his gaze burned into hers, his voice was tender. "Stay strong."

Desperate was the best she could do. She shook as hard as Blakeley sobbed on their chase to the hospital's Emergency entrance, and it didn't make it easier that Blakeley wouldn't take her eyes off her.

"W-what will they do, Mommy?"

"Make you better, darling."

"Are they gonna cut off my hand?"

"Oh, no, precious." But she was stealing herself for the inevitability of stitches.

Due to Blakeley's tender age, the doctor on duty insisted Devan come into the examination room to help reassure her. It was a request that didn't need asking; nevertheless, this was the hardest thing she'd ever done, and would gladly have traded places to save her little one this trauma and pain.

Emergency units and rooms were traumatic enough for injured adults who were conscious but needed them; to a child they were probably like their worst imaginings of what a torture chamber looked like. And then came the frustrating procedures, such as paperwork and the need for insurance cards to be run off...all the while Blakeley was surrounded by machines that had to look like monsters to her.

For the better part of an hour they sat and waited again, until finally the intern who had first examined her instructed she be moved to a different room.

"We're going to have to do stitches," he told Devan.

At that point, Devan's heart plummeted and her knees grew weak. And when they made it to the other room and the doctor approached Blakeley with the initial needles to deaden the area, Devan thought she would faint from her baby screaming, "Oh, no, Mommy! Nonononooooo!"

Devan used her body to block her daughter's view of what was happening and shakily cooed to her. "All right now...think about this, love...we're going to have Mead go to the store later. He's going to get the sugar cones you love, and every one of your favorite flavors of ice cream. You think about which ones because he won't know. We'll have to teach him about ice cream."

Inside, however, as her child sobbed on, Devan wondered if she herself could ever look at another sweet again without choking, without remembering this horror of a night?

When she finally returned to the waiting room with a limp Blakeley in her arms, a pacing Mead rushed to her and carefully took the child.

"The chief came to see how things were going." He nodded to his right.

Struggling to hold her emotions in check, Devan brushed tendrils sticking to her forehead and belatedly realized that somewhere between here and the square she'd lost her hat. Now her French twist was beginning to come apart, and no doubt she looked like a fool in her costume, but she was too drained to care.

"Sorry, Chief, I didn't see you."

"You've all been through a terrifying ordeal. How's the little one?"

"Seven stitches in that tiny palm." Her voice broke. "Who would do such a thing?"

"We're doing our best to find out. The good news is that the group sponsoring the candy giveaway kept extensive lists regarding who donated what as protection against exactly such an event. At the least, our list of people to interview will be narrowed extensively because we'll know who gave that brand of chocolate bar." Glancing toward Mead, he drew Devan aside. "I also want to give you hope that this was a random thing rather than a targeted one. Under the circumstances I'm sure you worried."

"Frankly, I haven't gotten that far yet, but I'll bet Mead has." She watched him rubbing Blakeley's back and her heart swelled at the soothing, protective gesture. Blakeley sensed it, too; otherwise she would never have let him hold her at a time like this. She not only let him, she was resting her head on his shoulder in the same relieved and trusting way Devan had when exhausted. Blakeley's heavily bandaged hand lay limply on his other broad shoulder.

"If it counts for anything, I'm rooting for you three," Chief Marrow said. "Now go home. Anything comes up, I'll holler. Don't you hesitate, either."

"You're very kind. Thank you so much."

It was a relief to get outside and breathe fresh air, but

concern for Blakeley's lighter attire had Devan slipping out of her vest as they headed for the truck. It wasn't much, but she covered her with the bit of suede.

"I have a blanket in the truck," Mead told her. "Lavender chased me down and took it from her car."

"She's going to be a great mother someday."

"You *are* a great mother."

Feeling her emotions getting the best of her again, Devan couldn't reply, and was relieved to see that they had reached his truck. Getting Blakeley comfortably settled took a little doing, as she was already half asleep from what the doctor had given her—the strongest pain relief and sedation he could risk for a child. Sitting her up to where they could fasten her seat belt wasn't working, and in the end, they agreed it was wiser to lay her down in the back seat and cover her fully with the soft wool blanket.

"I'll drive slow," Mead assured her as he keyed the engine. "Try to lean back and close your eyes. You don't realize it, but you're practically in shock yourself."

"If I do that, I'll think of Connie and Jerrold again. I'm torn about whether to phone them or wait until tomorrow."

"It's after ten, Devan. They're probably asleep. Give yourself a break and a few hours to regroup. Speaking from experience, pain medication and sedation is so-so and you could well have a rough night on your hands."

"Oh, God. I know."

At the house, Mead carried Blakeley inside, but quietly retreated to let Devan get her out of her bloody costume and into pj's that were easiest to put on and wouldn't irritate her bandaged hand. Through the slow process, Devan spoke softly to her, promising another Halloween pumpkin of treats and praising her for what a brave girl she'd been.

Only when certain her child had slipped into a deep

sleep did she kiss her a last time, turn on the intercom and close the door behind her. She carried the bundled stained costume to the kitchen where she found Mead pouring her a glass of wine.

"You had more white than red, so I guessed that's what I should open," he told her.

She dropped the clothes into the plastic-lined bin wishing she could do the same with the memories preying on her mind. "Thanks...but do you know what I want more?"

Without hesitation, he put down the bottle and came to her, enclosed her in his arms and held her close. "Ah, Devan. I'm so sorry. If I could have had the power to spare her..." He rubbed his cheek against her hair.

Did he seriously agree with the chief that it was possible his mother might be behind this? Devan leaned back to search his face. "How could you? No one could know what child would pick which candy. Besides, she prefers dark chocolate like I do, and I think most kids prefer the lighter sweeter stuff. Anyway, few know that detail."

Mead pulled her against him again. "You're probably right."

The sound of the doorbell had them looking at each other.

"I'll get it," Mead said. "Maybe the chief found his man already."

"More likely it's Lavender and Rhys," said Devan. "I said I'd call and I completely forgot."

Neither of them got it right. It was Connie and Jerrold Anderson and the instant they saw Mead, their expressions went from soured to indignant.

"What's he doing here?" Jerrold demanded. He urged Connie ahead of him and as far left as possible, as though Mead was a menacing pit bull straining at the end of its leash.

"*He* can speak," Mead said. "The question is, can you behave and treat your daughter-in-law with respect?"

Devan quickly came forward. "Please, let's keep this conversation as quiet as possible. Blakeley's exhausted and sleeping."

"When were you going to tell us?" Connie's tone echoed her husband's and as she belatedly noticed Devan's attire, she lifted her eyebrows with disapproval.

Devan managed not to look down but knew that without the vest, the form-fitting leotard covered her all right, but left little to imagine about her feminine form. "Tomorrow morning. Surely not when you're already in bed and don't need the stress."

But now that they were here, Devan shared what had happened, and praised the police for their excellence in taking evidence to find the guilty party. Nothing she said changed the unyielding expressions on their faces.

Jerrold snorted. "If they're looking for suspects, I'd suggest they stay focused in your backyard…or closer." For his part, he had yet to bring himself to actually look at Devan. Acting as though he'd caught her in her underwear, he turned back to the door and muttered, "Come on, Connie. There's no good in this. I told you so."

While she was grateful that Mead only fisted his hands at the innuendo, the scurrilous remark pushed Devan past her point of tolerance. "You know what would be novel, Jerrold?" she asked. Her voice quaked with pent-up emotion, but he wasn't the only one who was going to speak his mind tonight. "Just once I'd like to see you having the courage to insult someone—correction *me*—straight to my face."

"All right." Turning back, he pointed the unlit pipe he'd been clenching between his teeth at Mead. "It's a pity that his mother has more courtesy to inform me about the welfare of my granddaughter than does my son's wife. There, I said it."

Devan exchanged glances with Mead. So Pamela struck again, not only gambling that Devan might not be quick to phone her in-laws, but that Mead would still be here.

"The only thing you've said is that you're gullible to manipulation," Mead said, his voice low but rich with revulsion.

When Jerrold failed to reply, Connie approached Devan. Sadly, there was none of her usual warmth and reassurance in her manner. Her expression was brittle and her tone condescending.

"I think it would be best if you went and packed a few things, and you and Blakeley come be with your family. You're a good girl. We know that."

"I don't think you do," Devan murmured, slowly shaking her head. She felt as though she was seeing them clearly for the first time, not as she'd wanted them to be. "Even if you did, you couldn't encourage me to believe it, because your actions speak so much louder than your politically correct words.

"For the record, I'm a woman, not a girl, a *single* woman who earns her own living and is more than capable of making her own decisions—and that includes who I want in my life. Mead—" she gestured toward him "—has been nothing but respectful, generous with his time, and invaluable to us at Dreamscapes. Most important, if not for his quick reactions tonight, Blakeley would probably still be at the hospital, maybe in need of a transfusion. I think, Jerrold," she said quietly, "you owe him an apology. Frankly, you owe both of us one."

They didn't get it. Without another word, Jerrold took hold of Connie's arm and her in-laws left as abruptly as they had arrived.

"Well," Devan observed as Mead locked up behind them, "on the positive side, I suppose there is comfort in knowing where I stand."

But when she returned to the counter and reached for the glass of wine Mead had poured for her, it spilled due to her shaking hands. As she ripped off a paper towel to wipe it up, Mead came behind her and put his arms around her.

"Isn't that just like her to leave no germ unfertilized?" he drawled.

Realizing he was referring to his mother calling her in-laws, Devan managed a shaky smile, but she didn't reply. Her mind was racing forward to how tonight's conversation—or lack thereof—would taint her relationship from here on with the Andersons. And how would this affect Blakeley? They had a long wait coming if they thought she would expose her little girl to such prejudice, let alone allow her to be used as a pawn.

Sighing, Mead pulled a dangling hairpin from her hair before it could fall to the floor, then he began to gently remove the rest and set them beside the glasses on the counter. "You have every right to hurt, my sweet. But don't you dare feel like a failure." Finished, he smoothed the silky mass behind her shoulders and planted a kiss just below her left ear.

As his arms came around her waist again, Devan, thrilled to hear that endearment, leaned back against him and placed her arms over his. "Am I that transparent?"

"Only to me, I suspect. We're soul mates. Haven't you realized that yet?"

Dear heaven, he was going to turn her into a broken faucet. "I've been too busy lusting after your body," she managed to quip.

Rather than laugh, Mead turned her and framed her face with his hands. His gaze held hers and his thumbs stroked the shadows under her eyes.

"Try again."

Her eyes burned with tears of joy...but also tears of anger and hurt. "Oh, Mead...they didn't even ask to see her. She's their grandchild! They want her like a...a possession or a trophy, just as they wanted to take me from you to prove they can. But did you see? They didn't so much as go back there to look at how small and beautiful she is, to see that awful bandage on her tiny hand or to feel if she has a fever or to whisper, 'Nana and Gramps love you.' How do I explain that to her when they don't come to see her tomorrow or the next day, and don't even send a card or some little get-well treat?"

"What makes you think you have to? She's a sharp little kid, Devan." On another sigh, he drew her back into his arms. "Never mind. You're assuming it's all downhill from here, but there's no reason to rush to resolve anything, let alone everything tonight."

Nevertheless, her mind was in the mood to try. "Do you think Pamela had anything to do with that razor blade? I mean, first she calls the chief, and then Jay's parents...clearly she's not only adept at setting us up, she enjoys it."

"It bears keeping in mind, but no, I think the chief is right about it having been random. The who didn't matter."

"Okay. Still...I felt so cold when she looked at us this evening."

"She's up to no good, that's for sure."

"Do you think she might try to encourage, even help Jerrold and Connie try to take Blakeley from me?"

"That powerful she's not."

"Mead, she is. You know she is." As Devan's angst grew, her words became more urgent. "Why wasn't I strong enough to keep you at arm's length? If she's not able to control you, she's not above—"

Mead silenced her with a kiss. Not just any kiss, but a whole body, melt-your-bone-marrow kiss that soon had Devan whimpering yearningly and clinging tightly to him for fear of puddling to the floor. His own physical response was equally fast and profound, and his eyes burned with deep fire as he sank his hands in her hair and pulled her head back to speak.

"No more, do you understand? Doubt is exactly what she wants to put into your mind, what all three of them want. You look at me and tell me that you could trust their words more than you trust mine, that you want them in your life more than you want me—and I'll walk out that door. But for you, Devan, only for you."

"No!" The mere thought sent an excruciating pain piercing her heart and she pressed her face against his pounding heart. "I'm such a coward."

"You're the bravest person I know. I'd be the coward trying to get through tomorrow without you, never mind walking out that freaking door." Mead pressed a kiss into her hair and another at her temple. "Just hold me, Devan. Take any and all strength I have. And tomorrow we'll work on seeing that she trips herself up in her own plans."

As it turned out, concerns about Pamela were temporarily put on a back burner when the following day the razor blade culprit came forward—or rather, his mortified parents did. The Mount Vance high school student with a history of juvenile delinquent behavior had decided it would be fun to sabotage the candies donated by his mother and her sewing club. Chief Marrow confirmed that they'd located three other blades; fortunately, though, there were no other injuries.

The teen's father came to Devan to personally apologize and offered to pay Blakeley's hospital bill. Devan gave him her insurance agent's phone number and thanked him for the assurance that his son would be shipped off to military school as soon as he served his juvenile court sentence.

As for Blakeley, Lavender suggested Devan leave the cot at Dreamscapes and the child could stay there until her stitches came out and she returned to day care.

For exactly one day life seemed to get back on an almost normal track. Then came the phone call from Lavender that threatened to shut down their business.

"You're not going to believe this," she said in a loud whisper as she cupped the phone. "Sheriff's department deputies just came by and took little Eduardo away. Nina is in tears."

Standing by her SUV across town, Devan struggled to understand her friend. "What? Why? Does he have a record?"

"No, INS is doing a round-up, and his ID is bogus. You've got to get Jorges to get Manuel and Carlos out of town. I had no choice but to tell them where you were."

"Oh, no. What about Enrique and Pasquale?"

"Lord, Devan, you know the answer to that—they're dead meat. They're sitting ducks mowing at the wicked witch's place."

With all the commotion, Devan had forgotten what day it was. Her heart plummeting, she replied, "I'll get back to you as soon as I can."

Ending the call, she ran to Jorges and told him what was happening. They were only five miles from town and putting in a patio and garden for a new client. "Hurry, you need to take the boys somewhere besides your home. Tell them to find someplace they can lay low for a few weeks or so, then they can come back."

"Manuel has a cousin in San Antonio. We go."

Devan ran for her wallet and pulled out all the cash she had. "Here. That's for their salary and gas for you. You have to take the van, it's too risky to try to sneak back to get your truck. I'll have Nina drive yours home later so she and your wife won't be without wheels. Stay off the interstate as much as you can. Be careful."

Moments later, Mead pulled in with the patio stones. Seeing Jorges and the others leaving, he came to Devan. "What's going on? I could use the guys' help unloading."

"Sheriff's Department deputies are on their way here on behalf of the INS. Damn it, why don't they stick with the chicken or egg plants, the hen houses, or even the dairies? They know full well there are dozens at some and hundreds at others." She sighed. "Lavender said they'd already taken Eduardo."

Grimacing, Mead said, "Tough break."

"It gets worse. The other vehicle is heading out to Pamela's for Enrique and Pasquale. They're too far away for us to help them. But we will have to go collect our truck and equipment."

"When will Jorges be back? The best scenario would be to let him do it."

"Late tonight at the earliest. More likely tomorrow. There's no option, I have to go do it."

"Not without me you're not."

Devan had no desire to go anywhere near Regan property, but it couldn't be helped. She just prayed that this was one of those times when Pamela wasn't home. It would be exactly like her to be conveniently out of town and, therefore, appear innocent of prompting the INS to make a run on their business.

They stayed put, waiting for the official visit there to

give the peace officer permission to check their vehicles. As soon as he left, Devan and Mead stopped unloading the patio stones and drove to Dreamscapes, where she parked her SUV and rode with Mead to his mother's estate.

As she expected, the truck and trailer were there, but there was no sign of the young men. To make matters worse, the grounds were only partially mowed.

"Aren't there any high school kids or some unemployed guys looking for work that you can bring on-board?" Mead asked.

"It's high school football season, soon to be basketball season, and you know from the numerous corsages Lavender makes how this town is eaten up with sports as much as any other in the South," Devan explained. "Kids have no time to work. As for adults, I can't say there aren't any unemployed, but if they were interested, we wouldn't be hiring who we do. Look, why don't you go back and unload the rest of those stones and I'll finish this job."

"Sweetheart, I'm not about to leave you here by yourself."

"You don't even know that she's home. And surely she isn't going to do anything in front of her servants?"

Mead was resolute. "Just last night you were shaking remembering how she looked at you. Forget it. Besides, there are two mowers," he added, nodding to the far side of the grounds where the second, larger riding mower stood. I'll take that one."

"Oh, sure. Mead, if she sees you on a mower, she's likely to come out and shoot me."

"Look at it this way," he said with continued resolve, "the faster we get it done, the sooner we can get out of here and stop worrying about it."

However, Devan was soon proven right. When Mead began operating the larger mower, it wasn't five minutes later that a golf cart emerged from the back of the house. It headed straight toward him.

Mead let it follow him until he was by Devan, then he shut off the engine and faced Pryce Philo. "All right, let's hear it."

"Your mother would like a word, sir."

"As you can see, we're pretty busy. She couldn't give you the message?"

"I was sent to retrieve you."

"Well, since we both have a good idea what she's going to say," Mead drawled, "let's consider it said and leave each other to our work."

The manservant looked pained. "In that case, I'm to tell Mrs. Anderson something." He looked at Devan. "I hope you appreciate I'm only the messenger. 'You're fired.'"

"Fine," Devan replied. Frankly she'd been expecting that for ages, and as costly as it would be, it was somewhat of a relief, too.

"The hell it is."

Mead climbed off of his mower. As soon as Devan realized what he intended to do, she sprang off of her machine and, as Mead settled beside Pryce Philo and the cart took off, she stepped onto the back of the cart and sat on the rear seat.

"Stubborn little—" Mead turned to scowl at her "—you don't need to hear this. Haven't you suffered enough for one week? For one lifetime?"

"You misunderstand," she told him, surprisingly at peace. "I simply want to be there as a physical reminder to you that you have a reason to stay alive and out of prison."

Philo cleared his throat. "Mrs. Anderson, excuse me for interrupting, but how is your little girl?" At Mead's narrow-eyed look, he added, "I read of it in the paper."

"Thank you for asking, Mr. Philo," Devan said, hoping

he would pass on what she was about to say. "She's been in considerable pain and we won't know for a while yet whether she can resume taking piano lessons, or if there's permanent nerve damage."

"That's...disconcerting. But they've identified the young culprit responsible?"

"They have."

"At least that's one less thing to worry about," he murmured under his breath.

"Excuse me?"

"I was just extending my sincerest wishes for your daughter's full recovery."

"Thank you."

Philo drove around back where Pamela stood at the living room's French doors. When she saw Mead wasn't alone, she looked anything but pleased.

"What is the meaning of this, Philo? I gave you a clear directive. I wished to speak to my son. No one else."

"You don't have to speak to me, Mrs. Regan," Devan said with equal coldness. "I certainly don't care to speak to you."

Pamela's dark eyes flashed. "Mead. Please come inside. What I have to say is for your ears only."

"Anything you care to say to me, you can say in front of Devan."

"This foolishness has gone on long enough." Pamela pulled the ivory chenille shawl tighter around her sage-green suit. "I will not have you driving around out there for all the world to see. You may find it routinely amusing to besmirch the family name, but I do not. Either you desist immediately, or your little friend here will lose my support. From the looks of her reduced employment roll, she won't be able to fulfill her obligations anyway, and I must put the appearance of this estate first."

Once again Mead stared hard at her. "Good God," he murmured. "You are diabolical." He turned to Devan. "There's the reason the deputies were encouraged to collect your people. The question is," he asked, facing his mother again, "who owed you a favor you hadn't already collected?"

Pamela lifted her chin. "Don't be ridiculous."

"You know what, sweetheart?" Mead said to Devan, although he continued to stare hard at his mother.

"I'm afraid to ask." Devan knew she'd been right to insist on coming here with him. His strange tone worried her, and he certainly wasn't being wise in using that endearment. At the same time, she couldn't believe her ears—did he really think Pamela had done that?

"Suddenly, I'm glad you ignored me and came along, after all."

"It's certainly been educational."

"Take a good look at her, Pamela," Mead continued. "You can try to ruin her business, you can have her employees driven away every month, and you can call her former in-laws and spread all the poison you want. You'll just convince me all the more that this is the woman I want to spend the rest of my life with...if she'll have me." Mead turned to Philo. "You can return us up front now, if you don't mind."

## Chapter Eighteen

Mead noticed that Devan was unusually quiet when they returned to the mowers. After she politely thanked a grim-faced Philo for the ride, he watched her hop off the cart, then with an expertise he admired, she efficiently drove her mower onto the trailer.

As soon as she shut it down and began to tie it to the trailer, he touched her arm, only to have her shrug him off. Seeing the twin spots of color on her cheeks and her over-bright eyes, he knew he'd done something big-time to upset her.

How? All he'd done is declare his love and intent. After last night, how could she mind that? It certainly couldn't be a surprise.

Before he was able to help, she had the second mower on the trailer. He did snap himself out of his stupor fast enough to tie down one side of the mower, then—not to let this go on—he cornered her against the side panel of his truck. "Devan, wait. What is it? What did I do?"

"Could we not have this discussion in your mother's driveway?" She kept her eyes firmly planted on the second button of his plaid shirt. "I've already been forced to share what should have been the happiest day of my life with her. I do not think she's entitled to see how much I resent that."

Mead winced. Is that how she saw it?

*Of course it is, you fool.*

Thinking he should hit his head against the truck cab if it would knock some sense into him, he gave her time for her escape. She quickly ducked under his arm and hurried to the van to take everything back to the nursery.

Mead hopped into his truck before she left him behind. By the time he turned onto the road, he reached for his cell phone and keyed in the number for the florist.

"Lavender," he said as soon as Devan's friend and partner came on the line. "I've been an idiot and need your help."

When Devan's cell phone sounded, she checked the number to see who was calling. To her relief she recognized the florist number and not Mead's. Good, she thought. She was dealing with too many warring emotions to speak with him yet, especially over the phone. Driving and talking on a cell phone was dangerous enough.

"What's up?" she asked, hoping it wasn't another dose of bad news. She didn't think she could take much more.

"Are you close to finishing up there?" Lavender moaned. "Please, please, say yes. I need you to do me a favor and stop at your house before you return here."

What on earth…? "Actually, we're already on our way, but I'm hauling this clumsy long trailer," she told her friend. "You know it's a handful on turns and my road is narrower than some. The boys are gone, Lav. It's all a mess. What do you need that can't wait?"

"It's for Blakeley. I managed to spill orange juice all over her clothes and I need to get her changed. I'm so sorry to add to your headache."

"In this case, our headache. Make that plural," Devan said as much to remind herself as her friend. "Well, at least your timing is perfect, I'm only two blocks from the turn. Does she need anything besides the outfit? How's she holding up? Any sign of fever? Are the Children's Tylenol doing the job against pain or does she need that stronger stuff?" The doctor had advised that, if possible, Blakeley should avoid taking them, and Devan agreed wholeheartedly, concerned with possible negative side effects that might surface down the road.

"She's doing just fine. She's blowing you kisses as we speak."

"Kiss her for me. See you—oh, drat, don't follow me."

"What?" Lavender asked.

Devan's finger was already on the disconnect button. "Nothing. See you shortly."

With one eye on the rearview mirror, Devan completed the turn and continued down the street. She had hoped Mead would continue on to the nursery, or better yet go to the other house and resume unloading the patio stones. She wanted some time to think. No, she amended with brutal honesty, she wanted this morning never to have happened, not to her or any of the others. Most of all, she *wanted* not to have been so petty and snapped at Mead the way she did. But it mattered, damn it.

Hoping she could get inside, grab the outfit, and get out before Mead misunderstood and followed her, she pulled up to the curb in front of her house and killed the engine.

Then she ran to the porch and unlocked the door. It was the alarm keypad that cost her precious seconds. Before she could punch in the code, Mead had his hand on the door to where she couldn't push it shut.

"I just need one thing for Blakeley and then I'm out of here," she told him. "Please don't—"

"You don't need the clothes," he told her. "I asked Lavender to help me."

As she stared at him, it sunk in. "You used my partner to trick me? My best friend?"

"She's on our side. She wants us to have a few minutes alone." He closed and locked the door.

"Don't do that." Devan pointed—until she noticed her hand shook. "Open it up again."

Instead he stepped toward her. "I told her I'd been a jerk."

"You shouldn't say that. You're just not realizing that now there's no reason for Pamela not to come at us with everything she has."

Suddenly Mead relaxed…and smiled. "That's sweet. You're defending me again."

"Of course not." In that same instant she knew she'd stepped on a verbal trap door. "I'm—I'm…this isn't fair."

"You're right. I was selfish. I wanted you to know how much I love you. I wanted her to see."

All Devan knew was how difficult it was to avoid his riveting gaze. He wouldn't stop looking at her in that mesmerizing way, and no matter what words were exchanged, her body responded as though he were whispering in her ear, caressing her neck with his lips, his hands beginning their own possessive exploration.

Her mouth drier than a cut Christmas tree in February, she said, "It was my—*our* moment, Mead. Regardless of how much I protested early on, from the first time you kissed me again, I knew I'd been waiting for you to find your way to this moment."

He swallowed and nodded. "I'm so glad because as I keep telling you—the moment I saw you in the park, I knew deep in my gut that we belonged to each other. At the same time I was aware that unless Blakeley liked me, unless I could reassure you that I could be trusted in your lives, I might make you want me again, but you wouldn't give me your heart."

"That's right. You did. And I have, against all odds."

"Then I'm forgiven?"

"You know you are, but...oh, Mead. Lots of people fall in love and nothing comes of it."

"Something definitely will for us." Mead closed his eyes. Opening them, he asked, "Will you let me touch you now?"

More miserable without his strength and warmth around her, Devan simply stepped into his arms.

Scooping her up, Mead claimed her mouth with his, a sexy growl rising from deep in his throat. "Don't scare me like that again. I need this. *You*. Either we settle on some date or I go to that B and B."

Devan grinned against his lips. "You've barely proposed and you're threatening me?"

"I'm begging and you know it."

"The kitchen table is straight ahead and empty."

Mead's chest rose and fell on a deep breath. "Is Bev in need of fresh gossip and taking Jacque for a nooner?"

"Okay, so the coffee table is closer."

"Your mailman is just back from quadruple bypass heart surgery. Have pity." But as he nibbled at the sensitive skin along her neck, he added, "How about my room?"

"Lavender does deserve to be punished for five more minutes."

Mead groaned. "Five. Is that all?"

As he let her slide down his body, she wriggled away and started backing into the hall. "We'll be ruthless and make it fifteen," she said, plucking open the buttons on her shirt.

When she exposed that she wasn't wearing a bra, he lowered his head and strode after her. In the guest room she hopped up on the dresser. He hesitated a mere second before stepping between her thighs and angling his head for another kiss.

"Are you trying to refresh my memory again?" he asked, easing his hands past her denim jacket and into her flannel shirt to cup her breasts.

Devan let her head fall back and moaned softly. "No, inviting you to experiment with your own creativity." She shifted forward and wrapped her legs around his hips, drawing him closer. As he continued to stroke her with his calloused fingers, she plucked at the buttons of his shirt. But when she reached for the buckle on her belt, he gripped her wrists.

"Let me," he said.

Leaning back against the mirror, she let him open her jeans, tug them down, then his own. His wholly engrossed expression alone had her inching forward to meet him. Ready. Willing. His touch had her nearly begging herself.

Sliding inside her, he murmured, "Devan."

She couldn't think. She couldn't breathe. "I've missed you so. For years, Mead. You can't know. You can't."

"I only have to look at you, watch you respond to me, and I understand. Trust me, I do."

She tightened her legs around him. "How?"

"I wish I could explain it." He took her hand and pressed it to his pounding heart. "It's just here."

"Then love me, and don't stop."

Sucking in a sharp breath, Mead began pumping himself into her. Rocking his forehead against hers, he gazed down to their joined bodies and suddenly accelerated to race them to their completion.

Lifting her into his arms again, Mead groaned and sought her mouth.

Devan clung to him, willing to go anywhere he was willing to take her.

"Ah, babe…there's only one thing that could be better." He lowered them onto the bed, and fumbled with the bed-stand drawer. Then he brought out a velvet box.

Devan stared. "You were serious. You *were* prepared."

"Marry me," he said, lifting the lid to let her see the splendor inside.

For the rest of that day and the next, Devan and Mead did their best to fulfill Dreamscape's commitments. Jorges brought some reassuring news—that Carlos and Manuel had been embraced by family down in San Antonio, but would welcome the chance to return when it was advantageous to all. Mead promised to make sure when that happened, he would not only bring them back himself, but initiate steps to work them toward naturalization, as someone had done for Jorges.

Inevitably, the lawn-care side of the business suffered; however, fall was racing toward winter and the rains had abated for the time being. Most of their customers were willing to work with them as they began juggling schedules.

Hurting them every bit as much as the loss of Pamela's goodwill was the Walsh Development account, something that looked increasingly like a loss even though Devan did everything but threaten to sue for debt still outstanding. Apparently nonplussed, Riley had yet to make good on his last bad check, and so they refused to honor the rest of their Walsh commitments. When she tried to get him on the phone, she got no reply and her only option was to leave a message with one of his girls.

By the first weekend in November his office stopped answering the phone, as well. Something similar had occurred before, but then they learned that Riley's secretary and the rest of the office staff ceased to keep regular office hours and finally none at all. The biggest uproar, though, started with the revelation that Mrs. Walsh had closed the house and had left town to visit relatives on the east coast.

Rumors abounded. Stories about larger debt than anyone first thought swept through town and beyond. Those who had invested heavily in Riley's success—bankers, lumberyards, electricians and plumbers alike—filled the coffee shop and cafés, the post office lobby and the sidewalks in between. It became apparent that, like many duped in the financial world of late, the greediest were the most vocal about his duplicity.

On that Saturday, Mead was misting the orchids in the hothouse and eyeing the root systems with studious fascination when he heard the door to the creaky glass and brick building squeak.

"Are you really that intrigued by the things?" a male voice asked.

Mead took his time looking over his shoulder at Pryce Philo. Now what? he wondered, his blood chilling. "It's a novel concept for me—nurturing."

"Your military brethren certainly have no use for it. But I don't blame you. Mrs. Anderson is a lovely woman."

"If you're trying to break bad news gently, don't bother. The only relief I'll feel is seeing your back heading out that door, so whatever you're here for, get it said."

Philo inclined his head in the faintest of bows. "If that's what you prefer. I'm here to tell you that your mother has left town."

Mead studied the man's clothes for the first time. He'd been too caught off guard to notice earlier that for once Pryce wasn't in his butler suit, but rather a casual wool sports jacket, cashmere pullover and dress jeans, all black, all obviously designer brand. Not the kind of outfit one would wear if trying to look subservient, particularly to a fashion plate like Pamela Regan.

"I take it I'm supposed to ask where and for how long?"

"Not really. I know that bridge is beyond burned. I'm here to assure you the peace of mind that should come with such a decision."

"Taking up prophesizing?"

"Let's just call it setting some things right."

How did a man who looked like he didn't have a soul, let alone a life, do that? "What things? Why should you do me any favors?"

"Because I was in the military myself. A long time ago." The older man shrugged at Mead's wary frown. "It was another time, a different war. I lost faith. Watching you pull through and turn things around for yourself triggered a conscience I thought I'd lost."

Mead thought about his résumé and wondered what else wasn't on there. "If you're that good at hiding your past, would I be wrong in assuming there are people who would be interested in knowing you're alive and well?"

Philo offered a negligent shrug. "They have enough on their plates, world conditions being what they are. Generally, I'm content to live and let live—unless provoked."

That was a non-admission if he'd ever heard one and it brought Mead's thoughts back to Pamela. For better or worse, she was his problem. "What have you done? Where is she?"

Philo raised his ringless hands as though surrendering. "As I said…she's gone. First she's off to Florida to visit friends. Then she's taking a cruise. A long one."

"Why aren't you going with her? You already know her demands and needs. Maybe there's even more in it for you."

"Alas, even if I was interested, I get seasick."

The thought of this disciplined man having any weaknesses was almost laughable and Mead didn't believe him for a moment. "Is this about Walsh then? Are they together?"

Philo fiddled with something in his pocket as though debating his answer. "No more. And what romance there'd been was overexaggerated on both their parts. It was a game they played. No, Walsh's passion is gambling. He's eaten up with it. Add his expensive tastes and high ambitions, and you probably can guess that he took her, as well as your lady and anyone else he could, for more than pocket change." Then he added almost whimsically, "I suspect he'll be doing serious interviews with the FBI and IRS soon…if his bookie's enforcers don't find him first."

Devan would be pleased to hear that. Hell, no doubt most of Mount Vance would declare it a community holiday. "How will Pamela cope without you?"

Philo eyed him calmly. "Sir, I'm counting on her ruing the day she ever hired me."

"Are you sure you should be telling me that?"

"Who better, because she was willing to use you whether you were one hundred percent of your former self or a vegetable. Remember that in the time to come."

Time…not weeks or days. "You're a hard man to warm up to, Philo. You say you want to help and all you do is tell me riddles."

With a brief chuckle, the older man reached into his pocket. "This is for you. It should fill some blanks. Not all, I'm afraid—life isn't perfect and your mother has been a busy woman—but enough for you and the delightful Mrs. Anderson to regain your footing and…toss some of the baggage to the four winds."

"You don't make a comforting fairy godmother any more than you do a prophet or Greek bearing gifts. Why should I—" Spotting the small recorder Philo held out, Mead hesitated. "What the hell…?"

"If you don't mind, I'd prefer you wait until I leave before you start listening to it. But I trust you'll get an immediate grasp of the whats and whys. There are a few more gifts included on there," Philo added with a curt nod. "If you're smart—and I think your mind is just fine—you won't spend the credit in one fell swoop."

Mead stared at the recorder. He'd never seen anything like it. State of the art, was his guess, which made the mysterious Philo…what?

When he looked up, Pryce Philo was halfway out the door. Mead would bet a Ben Franklin-faced bill in a heartbeat that they would never see him again, at least not voluntarily on his part.

Curious, skeptical, Mead pressed the play button…and heard his mother's voice.

*"Damn her, I wish she was dead!"*

## Epilogue

*Christmas Parade*

"I can't believe it! They found her in a coma on the ship?" Lavender all but squeaked at the news.

Devan shivered, and it wasn't because of the December breeze sneaking through her faux lynx fur vest and winter-white turtleneck sweater. As she and Lavender stapled the last of the red-and-green crepe paper to the city park stage where the parade would pass in review for the float contest judging, she updated her friend on the latest in the saga of Pamela Regan.

"Hush. I think one or two people in the county have yet to hear that one." In fact, "The Fall of Dame Pamela," as it was being called by the injured, offended and the plain old gossips, was almost putting Riley Walsh and his crimes on the back burner. "What's spooky is that the doctors are saying it probably wasn't Pamela's first stroke since she started the cruise."

After Mead played the whole tape Pryce Philo had given him a few weeks ago, he'd presented it to Chief Marrow, who had contacted the FBI. They had been trying to figure it all out ever since—including who the enigmatic Philo had been. One thing was for certain: he hadn't just been the sophisticated but humble servant he'd pretended to be. So far about all they had determined was that much of his résumé was fabricated, and his name had been lifted off a cemetery headstone in Boston. The agents agreed that he was probably ex-military, but hardly your average enlistee—possibly someone who had a sudden need for a career change, yet wanted to enjoy the good life in an invisible sort of way. A scoundrel—a con of the most lethal variety. That had the physicians at the Miami hospital where Pamela was currently cloistered doing every test possible to check for poisons or other explanations that might point to hostile action.

As for Riley Walsh, a warrant had been issued for his arrest. No doubt considering his cravings, he would be easier to find than the restrained Philo. As Walsh Development had tanked big-time, Riley had run. Dreamscapes might be out several thousand, but others were starting to admit to greater losses, including two strangers who'd come to town the other day looking very out of place in their rental car, extremely powerful, and not at all pleased to learn that Riley was nowhere to be found. Almost anticlimactic, early indications were that Pamela had loaned him into the six figures, proving her last hurrah as a political power player had been a pitiful "huh."

Devan felt badly for Mead, but he kept telling her, "If it frees us of that and them, good riddance."

"Well, excuse me if I sound cold-blooded, but I'm not sorry, either," Lavender said with a rare anger. "She may spend the rest of her days in a wheelchair having drool wiped from her chin, but she practically reduced plenty others to that condition just jerking our chains."

Unable to argue, Devan sought reason. "There's that. But what I don't think even Mead is thinking about yet is that for the next several months he'll need to go through all those files in that house and see what's there. He's afraid what else he'll find. You know he remembers nothing of his father except what she'd told him of how he'd simply dropped dead one evening."

"Oh…you think *she* had a hand in that?"

"There are things she says on Philo's tape…cold doesn't begin to describe them. I don't think she ever loved anyone but herself." Devan shrugged. "I think any bad marriage can drive you to a heart attack or worse, so I'm not jumping to conclusions. But I'm going to make sure Mead has all the room and time he needs to feel okay about things, even if it means postponing the wedding."

Lavender hugged her. "Are you kidding? That's what's important to him…what you've got in each other." She bit at her lower lip. "Do you think he'll change his mind about moving into the mansion?"

"Definitely not—and frankly, I'd hate it, too," Devan confided. "It'll be hard enough on him to manage it in her absence, but he'll do it for the remaining employees so they get paid regularly. If she dies, I'm sure he'll sell it."

"Well, it would have been fun having the wedding there—and for the nasty viper to know you were," Lavender said with a mischievous grin. "Heck, I'm just excited about doing a Christmas wedding. You're going to look luscious in that white-fur-trimmed gown Mead insisted you buy."

"The only reason I did is because you swore we could alter it into a decent cocktail dress after…for what I don't know."

Lavender patted her swelling tummy. "For me to borrow after this one presents himself and I lose all my weight."

In spontaneous Lavender fashion, she and Rhys were expecting a little bundle of joy come late August, and were also discussing reception dates. Currently, the plan was to have a big New Year's Eve party. They were leaving next weekend for Las Vegas to marry in one of the infamous wedding chapels—Mead's gift to them for their complete and heartwarming acceptance of him.

As Lavender went to return the staplers and the rest of the supplies to the van, Devan checked her watch and worried if Mead would make it in time to introduce the mayor elect after all? He and Jorges had gone down to San Antonio to keep their promise to bring back Manuel and Carlos. Dreamscapes was soon going to need to hire a few other workers, too, and Nina was lobbying for one of her friends at school, a Vietnamese girl who had voiced an interest in working in the hothouse on bamboo gardens and bonsai plants.

Devan started when one large hand and one small one covered her eyes. Laughing, she spun around and embraced Mead, holding Blakeley in his arms.

"I found him for you, Mommy!"

"You sure did." Tears filled her eyes as she looked at the man who owned the rest of her heart. "Welcome home."

"I love that phrase—and you," he said, lowering his head for a kiss.

"Mmm. I missed *that*. Did everything go all right?"

"Pretty well perfect except for how much those boys like to talk. They're worse than this giggle puss." He nuzzled Blakeley, who squealed in delight. "The guys are settling back in at the Lunas'," he continued. "Nina is plying them with questions about you-know-who. The place smelled as though her mother was cooking to feed them a dinner for every day they've been gone."

"Good." It was difficult for Devan to speak when just the sight of him stole her breath. "That sounds nice."

"Then you might want to consider heading that way later. We're invited for barbecued goat later."

"Oh. Oh, not those cute little ones?"

Mead smiled. "I figured you'd have that reaction and told them to go ahead and start without us." Mead glanced over heads. "So where's Walter?"

He was searching for Walter Gleason, Mount Vances' mayor-elect, whom he would be expected to introduce. With Riley's unspoken default in the race, a group of citizens, encouraged by Mead, had begun a campaign in the twenty-third hour to promote him as a write-in candidate. It was the first win of its sort in the county, maybe the state.

"He's behind the stage, hoping he doesn't have to introduce himself," Devan said. She touched his cheek. "Go put him out of his misery and we'll leave Lavender to monitor the rest."

After a questioning look, he put down Blakeley and did just that.

In another minute or two, she watched as he followed Walter Gleason up onto the platform in his travel-rumpled jeans, his leather bomber jacket and blue pullover sweater. Yet the way he carried himself spoke of the same integrity as the new mayor fifteen years his senior in equally casual attire.

"Ladies and gentleman," Mead began as he stepped up to the microphone. "I'm told I'm a native of this town and I rely on your eyes and word that this is so. Less than two months ago, this town was held captive by a power-hungry few who didn't have our community in their best interests, only themselves. I happened to be related to one of them so there was no reason for you to believe me when I heard the whispers among you as you kept mentioning the right person for the job of mayor and asked, 'Why don't you do something about it?'

"No, I don't remember Mr. Gleason any more than I remember my name. But you said he's an honest man and has matched his dollar to city dollar repeatedly for the good of this community and its needy. You said he listens before he judges. *You* said you would write in his name for mayor before you abandoned Mount Vance to crooks and thieves. And you did. It's now my honor to introduce the mayor-elect of Mount Vance—Mr. Walter Gleason."

Devan was still blinking away tears and beaming with love and pride when he returned to her.

"Was it that bad?" he asked, taking her into his arms again.

"It was exactly right. So perfectly you." Devan rose on tiptoe to kiss his jaw. "Let's go."

"Where?"

"Home. You don't believe I meant it?" she asked, leading him to the parking lot. "Lavender said we have two hours and then she's bringing Blakeley, ready or not. Rhys gets back from Reserve training by seven. She intends to look like a goddess when he arrives."

Rhys was a Reservist and Lavender knew exactly what that could mean for him. For them.

As they started for his truck, Mead stopped abruptly, brought her flush against him and buried his face against her hair. "He's been given his orders?"

"Not yet. But they've been warned." Devan drew in his masculine scent and felt another heady wave of emotion for this caring man. "And you keep asking why I love you."

She leaned back and smiled up at him. "Home, Mead. I've missed you so."

"Me, too…which is why I'll always rush back to you." Holding her close to his side, he led her to his truck…and their future.

* * * * *

**Four sisters.**
**A family legacy.**
**And someone is out to destroy it.**

---

## A captivating new limited continuity, launching June 2006

---

The most beautiful hotel in New Orleans,
and someone is out to destroy it. But mystery,
danger and some surprising family revelations
and discoveries won't stop the Marchand sisters
from protecting their birthright...
and finding love along the way.